THE CELESTIAL LIFE

A NOVEL

Sean Anderson

An Imprint of Sulis International Press

Los Angeles | London

Library of Congress Control Number: 2019911596
ISBN (print): 978-1-946849-60-1
ISBN (eBook): 978-1-946849-61-8
Second printing.

Published by Riversong Books
An Imprint of Sulis International
Los Angeles | London

www.sulisinternational.com

Contents

*This book would not have been completed
without the support and, most importantly,
friendship of Alex Johnston.*

DAY 0

For the first time, Jonathan Celestial possessed a human body.

He touched his brown hair, and then looked down at his red shirt and baggy pants that were created for him by the Star Keeper. Walking through Capitol Hill, he was moving away from the crater he made when he landed on earth. The awe and joy he was experiencing at having a human body went beyond words. For the first time, he felt truly alive. He turned to look at his hand, at the lines on it. His body was approximately 25-years-old. At least, that's what he requested. His eyes were brown just like his hair. Breathing in and out, walking, he felt an ecstasy just from the simple sensations of being.

For too long he was content to be a star, feeling down and dejected, living in a shadow of who he really was. The night sky was a dark and lonely place. Sure, there were plenty of other stars, billions in fact, but they weren't nice. They were unkind and thoughtless. He was on a mission. Jonathan was looking for a sense of purpose. Long ago, something traumatic and terrible happened to him, and it was his belief that on the planet Earth he would find the source of salvation he was seeking. So at long last he was making progress in his life, heading towards a destination, a goal. Now, he felt like he was free, free to be the truest version of himself.

A hard-working celestial body, Jonathan lit up the far reaches of outer space for the entirety of his youth, approximately one billion years. So for hundreds of millions of years, since graduating from the Star Academy, Jonathan was laboring, working towards the personal goal of his to find meaning in his life.

One day, during a thousand-year break, Jonathan approached his direct supervisor, The Star Keeper, who was rather on the grouchy side.

"Hello, Star Keeper," Jonathan said, his expression downcast.

The Star Keeper turned to face his employee quickly. He sighed. "What is it, Jonathan?"

"How are you on this luminous eon?"

The Star Keeper turned to yell at a nearby star "You call that lighting up the night sky? I don't think so, buddy!" Then he turned to face Jonathan:

"You know I don't have time for idle chatter. What is it, Jonathan?"

"Well, I have been thinking…"

"…And?"

Jonathan said, "I want to travel to Earth. I want to use some of my Paid Time Off to fall to Earth."

"I see. If I recall correctly, you have accrued…thirty days of PTO."

Jonathan's expression was blank. "Thirty days? Oh, okay," he replied.

"So you want to go to Earth. What do you plan on doing there?"

"Well, I was thinking I could give the whole human thing a try."

"You…you want to try being a human?" The Star Keeper appeared flabbergasted.

"Yes, I would like to fall to Earth, take on the form of a human, and search for something."

"Search for something. What are you searching for?"

"For purpose. For meaning. Most of all…for hope."

"Ah…the talk about hope again." The Star Keeper looked at Jonathan with a stern expression. It was no secret throughout the galaxies that, for a while now, Jonathan had been feeling depressed "Look, Jonathan. You received top marks at the Star Academy—"

"Yes, and I aced the Human Studies courses. I know all about humans. I know that they drink coffee, dance, and work. But there's a big difference between reading about humans and trying to be one."

"Yes, but Jonathan. Earth is a dreadful place. War… famine…environmental degradation…political corruption…need I go on? Being a star is much better."

"But how will I ever know that for sure unless I give it a try?"

"Just take my word for it," The Star keeper said. He started moving towards a group of stars who were chatting.

Jonathan said, "Look, I know we stars have learned a lot about humans from all the research and everything. But no one has ever tried being one. Why? I want to try. I want to find…I want to find out what it's like."

The Star Keeper was facing Jonathan now. "Look, Jonathan. I know it has been a difficult time for you. What happened to you those millions of years ago was… horrible to say the least. But trust me, there is no good to be found on Earth. Quite the contrary!"

Jonathan floated up above all the other stars. "Attention, everyone! I'm going to use my PTO to travel to earth and look for hope."

The other stars turned to look at Jonathan, and proceeded to make fun of him:

Looks like this star has burnt out.

What a dimwit!

Like you'll find anything. Guy could barely light up his own galaxy.

Jonathan looked at the stars mocking him and then looked away quickly. He was breathing quickly.

The Star Keeper sighed again. "What am I going to tell Sir Cosmos?"

Jonathan went back to his supervisor. "It's my PTO, and I get to choose how I use it. I'm going to Earth." Now he was feeling determined.

"Well, if you're going to go, I guess you're going to go."

Jonathan Celestial approached one of his only friends and comrade, The Sun, feeling inspired.

"Heard you're heading down there," The Sun said. "I've been working overtime right now. June is a tough time of year for keeping the planet lit, at least in the Northern Hemisphere. Anyway, I wish you all the best in your ventures."

"Thanks, Sun. That means a lot to me. Any advice for me?"

The Sun appeared thoughtful. "You know, I'm not sure. I guess…don't ever rule out being surprised by humans. They can be the most confounding little organisms. Trust me, I spend a lot of time serving them. Jonathan, I hope you find what you are looking for. I know that life hasn't been easy for you since—"

"I know," Jonathan said. "No need to talk about it now."

"Of course. There is no need to talk about it. But you do know that what happened to you implicates us all, don't you?"

Jonathan nodded. "I do."

The Sun smiled. "If you need anything, just reach out to the Moon or myself. We're here to support you."

"I have a question."

"What's that?"

"I am going to Earth. What part of the Earth should I visit?"

"I dunno, Jonathan. There's so many wonderful places. London's nice, I hear. At least that's what the humans are saying. Florida gets a lot of my attention."

"What about over there?" Jonathan was pointing at an isolated strip that was diagonal from Florida.

"Seattle?"

"Sure. Why not?"

The Sun looked concerned. "I don't shine there very often. So many clouds."

Jonathan smiled. "I don't' know why, but I have a feeling that, if I'm going to find something special anywhere, it's going to be there."

The Sun said, "Do what feels right. We are stars; we can't help but shine, no matter where we are! Don't forget to look up to see us at night, and if you ever need to, make a wish."

So, settled, Jonathan faced the West Coast of the country known as the United States. He began falling, and soon he was plummeting through the heavens at a high velocity.

With an explosive landing, a crater formed. He arrived. Jonathan, having gotten out of the crater, was walking. He turned around, and saw that somebody walking a dog was taking a picture of the crater with a small phone.

Having reached the top of a hill, Jonathan looked out at the cityscape. It was as though the entire city were in the palm of his newly-formed hand.

Joy was the emotion Jonathan felt in that moment, a blissful joy, for he was liberated of the oppressive, depressing place that was space, and was finally free to go out on his own. So, as he began his search, he was determined to remain upbeat and positive, to not let anything weigh him down. This, he knew, was a new start for him, a new chance at existence.

"Life is just beginning," he said to himself. No longer a star, he no longer felt down or dejected. His eyes were beaming, full of light. He wore a massive grin.

Day 1

Standing on top of the hill, Jonathan Celestial once more gazed out at the city. From his textbooks in his Human Studies classes he learned about a place called New York City. He remembered distinctly the pictures of buildings, the skyscrapers which rose up so very high, captivating the imagination. The city before him was no New York, but it did seem to be a nice enough place. In the sky were many clouds. Jonathan was able, faintly, to see his comrade, the Sun.

He walked down from the hill. All around him he saw things which brought him back to his studies: trees, squirrels, a pool of water, children and parents, dogs, and so much more. To see them in person could not be compared with reading about them in a book in a Star Academy classroom.

Instinctively, Jonathan put his hands in the pockets of his pants. He reached out his hand, and saw that in it he held what was a crystal shard, a celestial entity leftover from when he was a star. Glittering, shimmering lavender, the crystal shard was mesmerizing to behold. He looked around, and then put it back in his pocket.

Laughing to himself, he started to run. His lungs were filling with air as he crossed the street and forced a car to skid to a halt to avoid hitting him. No longer in Volunteer Park, he was in a neighborhood that was teeming with vibrant energy. Faster and faster he ran. Soon he was sprinting so quickly, that people were turning to watch him.

The thick door of a building opened and slammed Jonathan in the face. He fell to the ground and rose back up at once. People continued to look at what Jonathan did, in awe and horror.

"He must have been running 40 miles an hour!" a man exclaimed.

Evidently, there were powers, a sort of cosmic energy that was leftover from Jonathan's previous form, present with him now.

He walked up the street towards the open door. Inside was a bakery. For the first time he smelled fresh slices of pie, their scents wafting through the air. Never before had he tried pie. In fact, never before had he done anything he was doing. So he stood in the line that formed, much in the same way stars did when gathering for lunch, and waited until it was his turn to order

"What can I get started for you?" a man with plenty of acne asked Jonathan.

Jonathan looked over all the pies. He saw one that had slices of peach in it. He pointed at it jubilantly.

"Sure thing. Anything else?"

"I'd like a cup of coffee," Jonathan said.

"What kind?"

Jonathan thought about his answer. "The kind that gets you going."

"That will be $6.79."

Jonathan realized in that moment that he had none of this "money". Stars lived off rations and were never in need. Desperate, he reached once more into his pants pocket and pulled out the crystal shard.

"Will you take this?"

The barista looked perplexed and astonished. "I don't know...I..."

Jonathan broke the crystal shard with his hands, lifting up a portion of the original shard.

"Here, this should do. I can assure you it is quite valuable."

Panicking, the barista accepted the crystal shard, handed Jonathan his pie and coffee, and went to go find his supervisor.

Jonathan had a seat. What struck him about sitting in chairs was how uncomfortable they were. He stood up and had a bite of his pie.

"Incredible! Illustrious! Immense!"

People around the café were looking at him. Some customers were leaving.

Then Jonathan Celestial sipped his coffee.

"Horrible stuff. Tastes like plasma. And yet I want more." He felt his body shaking, a tremor in his hands.

Once more, Jonathan was feeling the joy of being alive hit him with full force. He trotted out of the front door of the café just as the supervisor was coming out.

"Who the heck is that?" the supervisor asked the barista.

The barista shrugged.

"This city…"

Jonathan continued on his way, back across the street, up the hill. Suddenly, he realized that he was hearing something with his ears. It was mesmerizing in quality, and yet calming. He took a few more steps and saw an elevated stage. On it, stood three youngsters who looked to be manipulating tools. It was then Jonathan remembered his reading about music, and he surmised that they were performing.

The crowd assembled was small, but people were very engaged with the music, nodding their heads, locked into the playing. There was a drummer, a guitarist, and a fellow playing a larger, longer guitar. On the big drum, there was a logo that said the name of the group:

Static Sea

In particular, Jonathan was captivated by the guitarist's playing style. He played arpeggiated line after ostinato line, occasionally stomping on the pedals on the ground with his foot. Jonathan only knew of these Italian terms because of his reading. Jonathan started to sway, waving his arms through the air in time to the music. He couldn't explain what he was doing; he was simply feeling the music. He smiled. The guitarist had short black hair and green eyes. Rarely did he look up from his playing. Rather, he was content to stare at the ground.

Hypnotized by the music, just happy to be out and enjoying a day of life, Jonathan stood and watched them play song after song.

Eventually, the band stopped playing. The members got off the stage. Jonathan ran over to the guitarist who had so strongly gained his attention. Eagerly, Jonathan called out to him:

"Stupendous! Superb! Staggering!"

The guitarist looked up and met Jonathan's eyes. He ran a hand through his hair.

"What do you want?" he asked Jonathan.

Jonathan was confused. He didn't want anything but to compliment the music that had moved him. He looked intently into the guitarist's eyes, and said:

"Your playing was wonderful. I really enjoyed it. Thank you."

The guitarist smiled for a brief moment. "Well, you're welcome."

"Would you care to discuss your music in greater depth?"

Now the guitarist was moving farther away.

"I gotta go. Thanks for the compliment, but I need to get out of here."

"Wait! What's your name?"

Just like that, the guitarist was gone.

Standing in the crowd in Volunteer Park, Jonathan was spellbound by the music. He stood for a while, attempting to process what he heard. The music took him to another world.

Curious of what else there was to see in this city, Jonathan walked through the park, into the Capitol Hill neighborhood. He was enchanted by how busy the streets were, how much taller the buildings were, how much faster the cars zoomed by in this area. On and on he walked, his white running shoes causing his new feet to ache. He went down a hill, crossed a bridge, and approached a university. Everything seemed to emanate the color purple, and there were young people everywhere. Jonathan walked up an incline, past a record store. He decided to step inside.

"How's it going?" he asked the clerk eagerly.

The clerk did not respond in any way.

Jonathan asked, "Do you carry any Static Sea?"

"Do we carry what?"

"Static Sea! They're my favorite band."

"I'm afraid we don't. But feel free to look around."

Disappointed they didn't have the band he just saw perform live, he walked outside. He continued to go up the hill. While stopped at an intersection, he turned and saw that the telephone pole was decorated with posters. There were many posters for bands, but Static Sea was nowhere to be seen.

Where was that guitarist? What was the secret to his magical playing? How could something that meant so much to Jonathan seem to not matter to others?

It was in that moment that Jonathan was seized by an idea.

Yes, it was a very good idea.

Looking up at the early evening sky, focusing his attention on one star in particular, Jonathan looked at this star and then closed his eyes, making a wish:

Hello, my name is Jonathan Celestial. My Star Number is STA7368228383. I would like to make a wish. You see, I am living life as a human, but I feel like I don't know what I am doing. I feel confused. Can you provide any clarity into the, um,

He turned and saw the posters on the pole.

Can you provide any clarity into being human, please? Thanks!

His eyes opened, he sat down on the patch of grass before him. A minute passed, and then he felt a vibrating sensation in his temple. Closing his eyes, he heard a voice whisper:

Hello, thank you for your wish. Your wish is important to us, and will be addressed in the order that it was received. For reference, your wish number is: 6352824438. You should hear a response within the next few minutes. Thank you, the Star Department of Wishes and Whimsies.

Jonathan kept his eyes closed, for he was drifting towards sleep, which he recalled learning about. It was a frightening sensation, to disappear from the world with eyes closed, so he resisted it. Then, his head began vibrating once more. He heard a voice whisper:

Hi Jonathan. So sorry to hear you're having a rough go of it. Being a human isn't easy. No star has ever chosen to spend time as one, but our teams of researchers, philosophers, and writers have studied them closely throughout history. I'm going to send you a book I think will help provide clarity, for I believe that is the word you used. I'm sending it now. Hope it helps! Sincerely, Troy from the Star Department of Wishes and Whimsies. PS: Please walk across the street.

Excited, he ran across the street. As he approached a bench, he realized that there was a package sitting on it. The package had a small parachute hanging from it. He picked it up. He read the cover. It was titled On Humanity. The book was thick.

Jonathan lay down on the bench. By now, it was dark as his friend and comrade the Sun had completely set. Reclined, he proceeded to read the introduction:

Humans are peculiar creatures. Prone to strife, discontentment, and struggle, they nonetheless possess a true capacity for great beauty. The experience of being a human is not an easy one to concisely summarize as will be done in this volume. The first, most fundamental truth to realize concerning the human being is the very finite nature of its lifespan. To exist for 80 years or less is a demoralizing, albeit intriguing, reality to engage with. Death, that is, the opposite of life, is everywhere to behold in human civilization, if in coded forms.

Jonathan yawned.

Many humans eat, reproduce, and eventually die in a predictable fashion. However, a select few realize their own finite nature and use it as a motivating force. Through the arts, sciences, and other avenues, these more aware humans…

"The arts!" He turned to the section on art:

Through music, painting, prose, and dance, among other forms, humans produce art, which stands as one of their most sublime modes of expression. Highly subjective, art has the curious capacity to bring humans together. Music in particular stands as a communal act, both in performance and consumption, it involves many people, and can connect both performer and listener to something transcendent.

Jonathan was thinking about the meaning behind this when he realized that he was starting to feel tired. He lay on the bench and enjoyed the June evening. It was not particularly cold.

For the time being, he knew he needed to find and meet the guitarist of Static Sea, even just to make his acquaintance. Jonathan spent most of his time as a star being a source of derision and mockery from the other stars. He didn't want to spend his time as a human alone, and so he thought this musician, this guitarist, was the perfect first friend to make.

But where to find him?

Most likely, it was a good idea to keep his star powers hidden. After all, if he wanted the most authentic human experience, then it stood to reason to keep those powers unused.

Also, it seemed sensible to look for shelter. He couldn't spend all of his nights on a bench. But for tonight, it would have to do.

So Jonathan's head swirled with thoughts. Eventually, laying on a park bench in the University District of Seattle, Jonathan experienced the respite of sleep for the first time.

DAY 2

Jonathan Celestial woke early as his friend and comrade, The Sun, was rising over the city of Seattle. A soft, yellow glow reflected off the buildings. He stretched his arms high up above his shoulders, a sensation that seemed only natural. The neighborhood was quiet; an occasional car sped by the bench he was seated on.

"Where am I to go?" he wondered.

First thing first, he knew he needed to find a form of shelter. There was no way he could spend his thirty days sitting on a bench. Humans lived inside of buildings, this much he knew. Stars, on the other hand, were content to float and move through space. He then would need to find a building that he could dwell inside. He craned his head and looked at the buildings around him. A few of them had signs that said "For Rent" and "For Sale". He walked up to the closest apartment.

Inside was a hallway, which led to a big room. Jonathan went into the apartment and realized that it was full of people. Unaccustomed to crowds, he felt that he was sweating. In space, there had always been plenty of room to move about. This was a whole different dynamic altogether.

Jonathan observed that many people were using what he remembered were called pens to fill out paperwork. He watched the way in which a man's fingers reached around a pen and gripped it, enabling him to write. Such a phenomenon mesmerized Jonathan. Jonathan walked over and continued to watch the man.

The man turned towards Jonathan. "Can I help you?"

"Yes," Jonathan replied. "I was wondering if you could help me find a place to lodge."

The man laughed. "You and every other person in this city, pal."

So Jonathan walked around the room, realizing that everyone was filling out papers. Some people were writing on small pieces of paper.

"What is that?" Jonathan asked, pointing at the small piece of paper a woman was filling out.

Annoyed, she looked at him. "A check," she said.

"What is it that you are checking?"

The woman walked away.

Jonathan saw, up at the front of the room, a man who was gesturing with his arms, pointing at things, and not filling out any paperwork. This fellow, Jonathan presumed, was the one who was leasing the apartment.

Approaching the man, Jonathan said, "Hello. My name is Jonathan Celestial. I would like to live here."

"Grab a form," the man didn't make eye-contact with Jonathan. "You'll need first and last's month rent upfront. You'll also need—"

At that moment a young couple came forward. The man opened his wallet and removed some green pieces of paper that had high numbers on them.

"Money!" Jonathan exclaimed.

Everyone looked at Jonathan.

"Get out," the man who was showing the apartment said.

Outside, discouraged, Jonathan lamented how difficult it was going to be to find a place to live.

"Do I even have enough money?" he held the crystal shard remnant in his hand.

Hi Jonathan. No, you most likely don't have enough money, at least not in this city.

It was The Sun talking to him.

What am I to do? Jonathan asked.

Don't be so dark about things. Lighten up! Say, I have something I want to show you. Why don't you head down to Pike Place Market?

What do you want to show me?

Why, it's a surprise! Go on ahead. I'll meet you there.

Okay.

Looking before him he saw a bridge that led towards a walking path. He followed it, the occasional cyclist or jogger speeding by him. He gazed at the shimmering water, a pure blue beneath, and breathed a sigh of relief.

For three hours, Jonathan walked, unsure what this Pike Place Market had in store for him, but going there nonetheless. He observed the way in which the buildings got taller, sleeker. Out of these structures walked, predominately, bespectacled, flannel-clad individuals who were sipping coffee. Jonathan saw a sign that read: "More Cloud Storage For Your Business".

Puzzled, Jonathan had no idea how a cloud could have even more storage than it already did.

Accustomed to a typical star being around 2 million degrees Celsius at its upper interior, Jonathan was struggling with notions of "Partly Cloudy" and "High of 65".

Jonathan was struck by how the road sloped, how the streets were busy with cars that honked and sped along. In the distance, he saw a sign that read "Public Market". Suspecting that he had arrived, he moved towards the sign.

Just as he was stepping towards a stand a fish soared through the air and nearly slapped him in the face. He looked about him and saw people taking photographs with cameras. The flashes of the cameras reminded him of how stars twinkled.

To his right there was a staircase that led towards neon lights. Below, there was a bookstore. Intrigued by the pensive quiet that overcame the store, he walked through, surveying a variety of books. He found a book that concerned Greek Mythology. Flipping through it, he encountered Helios, a god who personified the sun.

"Wait until Comrade Sun hears about this," he remarked to himself.

He left the bookstore and went towards a candy store. He assumed that, like the café, he would here need to pay using currency if he was to enjoy any of the decadent sweets. Nearby, a short, fat boy was crying as his mother led him by the hand out of the store.

"But I want it!" he cried.

Jonathan looked at the lollipops. He liked to imagine that they were small planets, hovering there on sticks. The truth was he could only imagine what such a treat tasted like. He felt confident that he had never experienced anything like it.

He went to the front of the candy shop and offered his crystal shard in exchange for a lollipop. The clerk promptly told him to leave and never return.

Outside once more, droplets of rain were falling on his head. The feeling of being lightly pelted by water made him happy. He held out his hands, looking at them carefully, and watched the droplets of rain fall from his hands onto the ground.

In the distance he heard the sound of a piano being played. It was a bluesy type of rhythm, the sort that made one want to nod in time to it. Here on Earth there was music coming out of every corner.

"What a wonderful thing!" Jonathan exclaimed. He proceeded to dance to the music. He waved his hands up in the air and stomped the ground quickly. In that moment, there was just he and the music. A trash bin, a newspaper dispenser, and a fire hydrant all proceeded to circle around Jonathan in a rapid motion as he danced. Pretty soon several dogs joined the orbit. A crowd was gathering to watch, dumbstruck, as Jonathan channeled his own solar energy.

"Who is this guy?"

"Mommy, look at that!"

"Cool!"

You should probably give it a rest, Mr. Star of the show.

It was The Sun.

Lowering his arms, Jonathan watched as all the things he attracted fell to ground in a series of thuds.

Did I do something wrong?

No, but you should probably leave. Here, follow my rays.

A beam of sunlight was shining on a nearby staircase. Jonathan ran down the stairs and followed The Sun's cues, crossing a street, until he approached a fence. Beneath, there was the water of Puget sound, an oceanic current of water that sloshed and tumbled to its own rhythm.

I'm tired of leaving places. I'm tired of running. I'm tired of being told I have to go. Here I am; I followed your lead. What did you want to show me?

Here you are, The Sun replied.

The clouds in the distance, at once, dissipated. Revealed behind was a range of mountains. Pointed, jagged, they pierced the sky majestically. Glorious, resplendent sunlight was cascading down the edges of the mountains, the sky a pure blue.

Jonathan stared at the view for a long time.

What do you think?

It's…I don't know what to say.

Nothing like that in space, huh?

Not at all.

Jonathan turned back to look up at the market and the buildings from where he was standing. An oceanic breeze, salty and tart, was blowing in his face.

What am I to do, Comrade Sun? I just can't figure this human thing out.

You will with time.

At that moment, the rays of sunshine grew even more luminous.

Remember: nothing brightens a day like…brightness!

Jonathan turned from the view of the sea and walked along the path, admiring the views of Downtown Seattle. The buildings were predominately blue and dark blue in color, which made him think that the buildings resembled the water. In the shiny gleam of the skyscraper windows he could make out the water, breathing with life, beneath.

Walking by, holding a sign made of cardboard, was a disheveled-looking man, possessing a beard and thick, greasy hair.

"Spare change?" the man asked.

Confused, Jonathan replied, "Sorry, I'm not following."

A man walked by and flicked a few quarters into the jar in the disheveled man's hand. It was then that Jonathan realized that this man had no home, no pillow to put his head over. Filled with compassion, Jonathan put a hand on the man. Frightened, the man stepped back, and Jonathan did likewise.

Jonathan walked away, towards a bench. He thought about the fact that there were these massive buildings, and yet it was still possible for someone to be without a home.

Looking back on the realm of the stars, Jonathan felt no fondness for that place. Particularly after thinking about what happened those many years ago, Jonathan wanted, desperately, to find his place among humans.

Jonathan opened his book and read:

> *Humans all want to find home. For some, home is a physical place, a locale, a structure. For others, it is a state of mind, a space in which a human can be at ease, be known and know others. One way or the other, it seems natural that all humans are drawn towards this place.*

Jonathan thought about what he read. He scratched his head, looked up at the mountains shimmering in the sunlight, and then back down at the book.

His thinking was interrupted when he looked up and saw a magazine dispenser not far off. He approached it, pulled open the door, and read through the section on local music.

To his joy, astonishment, and wonder, he saw that Static Sea were scheduled to perform tomorrow night at the Treasure Chest. This then was another chance to experience music, and perhaps to learn the name of the guitarist who was so talented. He ripped out the page from the magazine, put it in his pocket, and walked on his way.

Eventually he made it back to the place known as the University District. This was the neighborhood where the Treasure Chest was located, and for the time being, it seemed that it would serve as a decent enough base of operations for Jonathan. By now, his feet were aching from all the walking he did. Pain was not something he was familiar with.

You okay, Jonathan?

He turned and looked up at The Sun, who was beginning to set.

I don't know! My foot hurts terribly badly. Will it ever stop?

It's just a little pain. Try to get some rest, and it ought to be gone the next time I rise.

Okay. Hey, Sun.

Yes?

Thanks again…for everything.

Any time. If you need anything, I'll be back in 5 hours and 46 minutes. Direct all concerns in the meantime to the Moon.

But he's such a downer.

Yes, well, someone's gotta do his job. Not all of us can have dispositions that are…sunny.

Good one. Good night!

Good night, Jonathan.

Excited by the prospect of seeing Static Sea perform, tired and no longer afraid of sleep, Jonathan Celestial made himself comfortable on the bench, and soon was asleep.

Day 3

It was midday, and Jonathan Celestial was walking through the University District. He passed by Thai restaurants, stores that sold university gear, and eventually made his way towards the Treasure Chest.

There was a poster in front of the venue that showed the members of Static Sea sitting on a couch. They were smiling. The guitarist was laughing, his mouth open and his eyes bright.

Mitch Varner-Drums

Tim Crawford-Bass

Blaine Jaggerson-Guitar

So that was his name.

Jonathan walked towards the venue, as though he was going to enter, but a person behind the ticket booth told him that the doors didn't open for the show for five hours.

"Can I buy a ticket?"

"Sure. $10, please."

Jonathan reached up with his crystal shard and handed it to the vendor."

"What the heck?"

"Oh, sorry." Jonathan took back the crystal shard. His legs were shaking.

He turned around, away from the booth, and walked up the street. He started worrying about how he was going to acquire ten dollars. He knew it was imperative.

Jonathan walked up the street and towards the University campus. The buildings were stately and ornate, looking as though they belonged in another century. Everywhere there were students, young people, walking, carrying books and backpacks. Jonathan saw a poster that advertised Summer Quarter.

He kept walking, passing by the School of Art and then the School of Music. Inside, he could hear a French horn blaring away.

On and on he walked. His mind was racing. His hands were sweaty; his heart was racing.

Though he felt nervous, he knew he needed to choose to experience joy. Here he was, alive, free to walk as a human. He clenched his fingers in a fist and then put his hands at his side, walking with purpose and determination.

He passed by a series of trees. He reached out a hand and felt bark for the first time. Running his fingers against the tree, the texture was unlike anything he ever felt before. He continued to feel it, now with the back of his hand. He smiled.

He looked behind him and saw a sign that read, "Andrews Museum of Natural History."

Stepping up towards this building, he saw a tower that was comprised of wooden, painted animals. On top was a bird.

"What in the name of Sir Cosmos is this?"

Unsure of what it was, he entered the museum. Inside, there were paintings and pieces of artwork that, Jonathan learned, were from the Native Americans who once dominated the region.

"Beautiful," Jonathan said as he gazed upon a carving of a salmon fish.

Then he approached the front of the museum. A college student sat behind a desk, looking at his phone.

"Hello! My name is Jonathan Celestial. I would like to sell this." Out of his pocket he pulled out the crystal shard.

"I'm sorry," the employee said, looking up from his phone. "We only accept donations at the museum."

"I will give it to you for ten dollars. Okay?"

"Like I said, sir. Donations only. And if you're going to sell that, you might try raising your price. Think of it as free business advice."

"Twenty dollars?"

The employee went back to looking at his phone, apparently done talking to Jonathan.

Jonathan let his head hang low. Then he saw that nearby was a café. If there was anything Jonathan knew about being a human, it was that he liked coffee. He went over and sat at a table just so he could enjoy the smell of java that permeated the space. He reached into his pocket and pulled out the crystal shard once more. He looked at the contours, the edges of it. In the reflective sheen he could see his own face. He saw his brown eyes, his brown, straw-like hair. He smiled.

"Excuse me, sir."

Jonathan looked up and saw a man standing before him. This man wore a fancy-looking hat. He had a tie on and his sleeves were rolled up. His moustache was very long, Jonathan thought.

"Hello! I'm Jonathan Celestial. I will sell you this for…" he was thinking about the free business advice he received. "I will sell it to you for thirty dollars."

"Why, that's a great deal. That's a steal!"

"No, please don't steal it from me."

The man slapped down a twenty dollar bill along with a ten. "My name is Perry Jensen. I specialize in gems and crystals, and what you have there is wonderful. It looks out of this world!"

"You don't know the half of it," Jonathan replied.

So they completed the transaction.

Jonathan Celestial proceeded to pump his fists in the air in triumph. People in the café were starting to look at him. He walked up to the front counter of the café and used his new, legal, paper currency to purchase the biggest coffee they had. Seated, he sipped his beverage and felt the jitters once more.

Outside, he was walking down a slope away from the museum when a rotating disc flew towards him. He put up his hand, and the disc began to orbit him, floating around him in circles.

"Whoa! Cool!" a student was approaching Jonathan. His hands were outstretched as though he wanted the disc back.

Jonathan leveraged the gravitational pull to fling the disc towards the student.

"How'd you do that?" the eager student asked.

"Um…it's a long story."

"Wanna play catch?"

Jonathan looked up at his Comrade, The Sun. He was able to calculate that he had three hours until the concert.

"Sure. Let's play catch."

Back and forth they flung the disc. Jonathan would jump high into the air, being sure not to use his star abilities, simply catching the disc in his two hands. He threw it back and watched as the student ran to catch it.

"What's your name?" the student called. "I'm Arnold."

"I'm Jonathan Celestial!"

"Jonathan Celestial. Are you a super hero?"

"Not quite."

They continued to throw the disc.

"What are you studying?" Arnold asked.

"Life!" Jonathan beamed.

"I'm studying biology. So I am, too!"

There was a pause.

Arnold said, "But what's your major?"

Unsure how to respond, Jonathan said, "Astronomy."

"Oh, neat."

A little while longer they threw the disc, and eventually Arnold said, "I need to get going. Great to meet you, Jonathan."

"Yeah!"

"Maybe I'll see you out here again sometime."

"Sure thing."

Arnold took the disc and walked away.

At last: a conventional human-to-human interaction. In particular, Jonathan was pleased by his ability to hide his starhood.

Still smiling, he walked towards the Treasure Chest.

"Hello. I have ten dollars," he announced to the lady at the ticket booth. "In fact, I have more than twenty."

"Good to know."

She printed a ticket for him. He held the ticket in his hand and read the band's name. He stepped towards a fellow who was ripping the tickets of patrons and handing them back to them.

"Please don't rip mine!" Jonathan held the ticket close to his chest.

"Well, then you can't see the show, bubs."

"Okay, okay." His hand shaking slightly, he gave the man his ticket. He took it back and entered the performance space of the Treasure Chest.

It was a dim, big space. At the front was a stage with all the instruments out.

"Where is the band?" Jonathan wondered.

He was standing still when a man with long, shaggy brown hair bumped into him.

"Whoa, sorry my dude. I did not mean to collide with you."

"That's okay," Jonathan answered.

The fellow looked at Jonathan and smiled. "Good energy is coming from you."

Jonathan sniffed his armpits as a precaution. "Is it?" he asked.

"Yes, I can tell that you are pure of heart and virtuous." The man made eye contact and did not break it.

"My name is Jonathan Celestial. What's yours?"

They shook hands.

"Name's Dave. It may seem a simple name, but it brings with it balance and harmony."

"Interesting."

"Tell me," Dave said, "are you excited for the show?"

"Why, yes. Yes I am! I love the guitar work they do. I love the drum beats. I love the bass lines. I love this band."

"Far out!"

"I hope they're not far away!"

Dave put a hand on Jonathan's shoulder. "I didn't mean it literally. What I meant is…oh, never mind."

The two of them stood. More and more people were entering the venue. It was beginning to get crowded and loud.

"Do you like Static Sea?" Jonathan asked Dave.

Dave ran his hands through his hair. "Do I? I live for this band. What Static Sea promise is a journey, a voyage through time and space, filled with transcendence and bliss."

"Transcendence?"

"Transcendence."

"What does that mean?"

Dave paused and said, "It means everything and nothing."

Jonathan nodded thoughtfully. He was confused.

Then the lights dimmed and the band came on the stage. They got right into playing a lively number. It had a strong atmosphere to it, with intricate guitar playing. The drum cymbals swelled dramatically. Blaine, the guitarist, grabbed a violin bow and ran it against the strings of his guitar.

"Righteous!" Dave yelled.

The mood of the audience was tranquil, locked into the tapestry of sound that the band was creating. The music had no singing, but the emotion was still strong in it.

Dave leaned in close to Jonathan. "What does this music mean to you?"

"It means starting something new."

"That's beautiful. What are you starting?"

"I'm learning how to be a human," he said, with honesty.

Static Sea played song after song, but they all really bled together. A string quartet came out at one point, adding embellishments to the music.

"Where are you from?" Jonathan asked Dave.

"Seattle."

"Neat!"

"But my spirit comes from some place altogether different."

"What's a spirit?"

"It's…well, it's hard to explain."

This seemed to be the answer that Dave gave every time Jonathan asked a question concerning his beliefs. It was strange to Jonathan.

Eventually the band concluded their performance. The members of Static Sea bowed, walked off the stage, and disappeared from view.

"The reason they call it the Treasure Chest is because it is a place where valuable things are found, things that are life-giving."

Jonathan wasn't sure he understood what he was hearing, but he was excited when he saw Blaine walk by and address him:

"Oh, you, um, hello."

"Terrific! Phenomenal! Super!"

Dave put his hands in Blaine's. "Your show made my heart glow." He bowed his head. "Thank you," he whispered.

"We definitely messed up during the bridge of "#27".

"Friend," Dave said, "There is no messing up. Only exploration. It was a wondrous concert. I look forward to listening to your album on repeat. Thank you for the performance."

Blaine nodded. He turned to Jonathan. "Who are you?" he asked.

"I'm Jonathan Celestial! Your show was phenomenal."

"Nice name." Blaine reached out a hand. His grip was weak. "Blaine," he said.

A lull followed. Then Blaine said, "Well, you've made it to two of our shows. I guess that makes you our number one fan."

"I love your music. In particular, I enjoy your playing."

Blaine blushed. "Thanks." Blaine pointed towards the stage. "I need to tear down. I—"

"I can help!"

Jonathan hopped onto the stage and proceeded to take orders from Tim and Mitch. Once everything was put away in the van, Blaine said, "We were just going to grab some drinks. Do you want to join us?"

"Join you? I'd love to!"

They crossed the street and entered a bar where loud rock music was playing, the lighting dim.

Blaine sat down with a beer.

"I'll take a coffee!" Jonathan exclaimed.

Once more he was feeling energize as he sipped his drink.

"You don't drink?" Blaine asked.

"I like coffee," Jonathan replied.

"That's cool with me. So, you've been to two of our shows. I'm glad you like our music."

"I do! Your music is great!"

Blaine blinked a few times and then said, "You know, you're flattering me. Why don't you tell me about yourself."

"What about me?"

Blaine paused. "What do you do?"

Having finished his coffee, Jonathan said, "I do all sorts of things. I drink coffee, I run, I go to concerts. It's all wonderful."

"Do you have a job?"

"I….um….it's complicated."

"Fair enough. I work as a barista at the Java City in the U-District."

"Okay." Jonathan pretended to know what a barista was. After all, there were limits to his studies.

Blaine was running his finger around the edge of his glass. "Are you from Seattle?"

With tact, Jonathan answered, "It's the first place I ever came to."

"Very cool. You've probably seen it change a lot over the years. Originally I am from Oregon. So not too far off."

Blaine told Jonathan the inspiration behind the band:

"You know, I got out of college five years ago. I studied history. I always liked to play the guitar. I liked post-rock and shoe gaze music a lot."

"Post-rock? What's that?"

"It's what comes after rock."

"But what is it?"

Blaine sighed. "It's post-rock. It's dynamic, emotional, intricate."

"Sounds great!"

"Yeah, it is. I felt inside of me like I had these feelings, this vision, that I wanted to express. I wanted to create music that would make people feel wonder and awe towards life. I want to make people appreciate life more."

"Well, it certainly works. Already I feel myself appreciating it more and more. "

"That warms my heart, Jonathan. There' more to the story Static Sea, but I'll spare you the details."

"Okay. You know, I am looking for something myself."

"And what is that?"

"It's hard to describe. I'm looking for healing. Let's leave it at that."

Blaine chuckled. "You and me both, pal. Listen," Blaine said, "that was really kind and thoughtful of you to help us put away our equipment earlier. Our second album just came out, and we are playing shows around town to support it. Hopefully I'll see you again sometime."

"When's your next show?"

"Tuesday."

"Oh, okay…what day is today?"

"Friday. We are playing at the Igloo."

"You're playing in an igloo?! Sounds cold."

"Good one. That's what the venue is called."

Jonathan didn't reveal that he wasn't joking. "I will see you Tuesday at the Igloo."

"You know, Jonathan, you strike me as very genuine. It's refreshing, to be honest."

"You know what else is refreshing? Coffee!"

They stepped out into the warm city air. It was nearly summer. Blaine said goodbye, and they parted ways.

Jonathan walked down the slope, to the bench where he slept the night before. He reclined on the bench. He thought about calling out to The Moon, but decided not to.

In accordance with his search, he thought to himself that it might be a good idea, tomorrow, to find work. He imagined different roles and occupations. He thought it might be nice to be a barista, and so he imagined sipping coffee all day, getting paid to do it, until he was asleep.

Day 4

"Hey, Jonathan. What are you doing? Wake up."

Looking up, Jonathan Celestial saw the face of Blaine, his green eyes as bright as Comrade Sun above.

"I...um..."

"Were you sleeping here? All night?"

Jonathan nodded, feeling sluggish.

"So my number one fan is homeless. Who knew?"

"I'm sorry," Jonathan said. "I'm sorry for being homeless."

"Oh no, don't apologize. Look, it's..." he pulled out his phone and looked at it. "...It's ten-thirty. I was just out on a walk through the neighborhood. Why..." Blaine looked around, as though he was wondering if anyone was watching them. "Why don't you come back to my place, at least for a shower and some coffee."

"Coffee! Okay!"

Blaine extended a hand. Jonathan took it, and sprang up off the bench.

"Do you have any possessions to bring with you?"

"Just my book."

"That book looks thick. You read the classics?"

Jonathan put a finger to his chin. "Not quite."

They walked up a slope, passing by student apartments. The Sun was high up above, the sky clear with the exception of a few clouds. As they walked higher up, Jonathan could see a neighborhood.

"Where's that?"

"Over there's Eastlake. And then there's downtown."

"Cool!"

They made their way up the hill, moving parallel with the campus. Cars were speeding by. Trees stood dotted the streets. Then they took a turn, walked down another street, made a few more turns, and were standing in front of a building.

The sign read, *Eclipse*.

"It's a silly name for an apartment, really..." Blaine was saying.

"No, no. Eclipses are lovely."

Inside and upstairs they stopped at a door at the end of the hallway. Blaine reached into his pocket and pulled out some keys. They jangled as he searched for the right one. Inserting the key into the door, he opened it.

Inside, Mesmerized by the mirror, he held out a hand and touched his reflection. It was a space that was immaculately clean. Paintings hung from the walls, which were painted a cheerful yellow. There was not a piece of garbage or clutter anywhere to be seen.

"Follow me and I'll set you up with the shower..."

For the first time, Jonathan took off the only clothes he owned. It was cold as he stood there. He held his arms close to his side. Once more he looked at his reflection.

Inside the shower stall, he turned the handle towards the label "C" and immediately turned to jump back, banging his head on the shower stall door. It took him a while to calibrate the temperature to his liking. After applying far too much soap and shampoo, not bothering to rinse, he stepped out of the shower, grabbed a towel, and dried off.

Blaine left out some clothes, neatly stacked, for Jonathan to put on. He saw Jonathan's hair and said, "Looks like someone likes to apply soap, huh."

"I do! Soap is a wonderful thing."

Blaine leaned against the door frame with his arm. "Look, Jonathan. I'm happy to host you for maybe a day or two, but this isn't a hotel. Just thought I'd lay out the terms early."

"A day or two? Fantastic!"

Blaine stepped into the main room of the apartment, which was sparsely furnished. "Today is my day off," he said. "You said your job situation is complicated. I take it you're unemployed?"

Jonathan answered, "Unemployed. What makes you think that?"

Blaine looked at him with a skeptical look and spoke in a dry tone. "You were sleeping on a bench."

"Fair enough, I suppose."

"Well, I'm all about empowering the disenfranchised, but I need to get going. I have a date today."

Jonathan walked up towards Blaine. He put his hands on his shoulders. "Won't you help me? Please? I'm no freak. Just…just a little lost."

Blaine looked around the room, and then said, "All right. I'll reschedule. I'll help you find a job. But regardless of what happens, if you don't find a job soon, we'll need to talk."

At Blaine's insistence, they sat at the table.

"So," Blaine began, holding a pen in front of paper, "What are you good at?"

"I dunno." Jonathan again put a finger to his chin. "I'm good at running."

Blaine stared at him.

"I'm also good at drinking coffee," Jonathan continued.

Blaine stared at the paper in front of him.

"You want to be a barista?"

"I'd love to!"

"Any prior experience?"

"No."

"Well, the barista game is pretty hard to get into, unless you want to go the corporate route. Tell me something. What do you like to do?"

Pausing to think, Jonathan raised his arms in the air and then proclaimed, "I like to express myself."

Then Blaine smiled. "You like to express yourself? I have just the idea..."

•••

Jonathan Celestial and Blaine walked through the heavy doors into the interior of the studio. The space was vacuous, a few lights shining on a table, which had a set behind it. Designed to look like a kitchen, the set was convincing enough. On the table of the set, there was a pair of pants with a stain on them. Nearby, stood a man wearing horn-rimmed glasses who was holding a video camera.

"You're just in time," he said to the two of them.

"Jonathan," Blaine began, "Meet one of my friend Rob's collaborators, Spencer Lindblom."

"It's a great pleasure," Jonathan said reaching out a hand.

"So here it is," Spencer said, handing the spray to Jonathan. "Take a look at it, what do you notice?"

"Very colorful. It feels nice in my hands, like I was meant to behold it."

"Yes," Spencer continued, "I daresay you indeed were meant to behold Gentle Koala Cleaning Spray in all its glory. Now, do you remember your lines?"

"My lines?"

"Yes, do you remember what to say?"

"Jonathan prefers to go with the moment, to see how things feel. That's his acting approach," Blaine said, staring at his phone.

"Very well. I'll get the camera ready," Spencer replied.

So Jonathan took the orange bottle in his hand and walked towards the set designed to look like a kitchen. There was a counter and a table with chairs. Jonathan had a seat at the table. He looked up at the lights which rained down radiant beams on him, took in a deep breath, and then went over to the counter. He ran his fingers along the hard surface of the counter, scrutinizing it carefully.

"Jonathan!" Spencer called.

"Yes?"

"We're rolling in 5, 4, 3, 2, 1…"

Jonathan stared directly into the camera, his eyes not leaving the lens.

"My name is Jonathan Celestial. I use Gentle Koala, and so should you."

"Cut!"

Blaine walked over and put a hand on his friend's shoulder. "Not quite, buddy."

"What's wrong?"

"Well, there's a whole lot more you need to say than just that you use it."

"What else do I need to say?"

"The purpose of a commercial is to convince people to buy your product."

"I understand," Jonathan replied. "I think I made a convincing case for using this product."

"I'm afraid you're going to need to try a little bit harder."

"What else do I say?"

"Remember what I told Spencer? You just need to get into the moment. The words will come to you."

"Got it." Jonathan looked determined.

Spencer pointed the camera at Jonathan and counted down again.

"Greetings. I'm Jonathan Celestial, and I want to tell you a story. In the beginning, there were the cosmos. There were planets, and stars, and the moon, too. After several billions of years, there were humans. Throughout history, humanity wrestled with spilling juices, greasy liquids, and other substances on its clothing items. All seemed to be lost…until one day. One day, scientists in the most secluded laboratory invented Gentle Koala Cleaning Spray, a spray that will blow you away. No longer were stains free to reign, ruining clothes and humiliating people. Finally, humanity had hope. With Gentle Koala Cleaning Spray, there was now a way to get rid of those cruel stains. Observe!" He sprayed the bottle two dozen times on the stain. The spray was dripping off the pants. "See for yourself. Armed with Gentle Koala Cleaning Spray, I can render this stain powerless. To finish the story, equipped with Gentle Koala Cleaning Spray, humanity entered into a golden era. Peace prevailed. No one ever felt pain or sorrow, because there was the shining light that is Gentle Koala Cleaning Spray. Purchase it today."

"Cut! What in the…"

Blaine walked over to Jonathan.

"No good," he said.

"What's wrong?"

"I…um…well, I just think it's a bit much."

"Is it?"

"And how many times did you say the name of the product?"

"I don't know…five?"

Spencer walked over, holding the camera at his side. "This isn't a spiritual experience. It's a cleaning spray for stains. Can you tone it down a little?"

"Sure thing," Jonathan said. "I will give it my all."

"Give it your all," Blaine said, "but give less of your all. Okay?"

Spencer counted off, and they proceeded to film.

"Hello. I'm Jonathan Celestial, and I hate stains. Stains are awful. Just when you think things are going great. Boom! There's a stain on your shirt. How terrible! Thank heavens there's Gentle Koala Cleaning Spray." He proceeded to spray. "See how Gentle Koala Cleaning Spray will neutralize even the most stubborn stain?" He pulled the spray trigger sixteen times. "Take that, stain!" Then he looked at the camera, his expression solemn. "Gentle Koala Cleaning Spray is worth every penny you have. Consider strongly the notion of purchasing some."

"Cut!"

Blaine walked over. "What did you just say?"

"Gentle Koala Cleaning Spray is worth every—"

"No, silly. I heard you. I'm just having a tough time fathoming how you came up with it."

"I said it, and I meant it."

"Okay, well you might like to try being a little less…I don't know…intense about it." Blaine grabbed the bottle from his friend. "It's half gone, for crying out loud."

Spencer walked over. "That was better," he said, "but it's still not quite what I'm looking for. Try again?"

"Okay!" Jonathan cried.

Once more the camera was rolling. Jonathan smiled. "So one day you're at a party, and then out of nowhere you spill grape juice on your pants! Enter Gentle Koala Cleaning Spray. Check out how it gets rid of the stain." He sprayed the bottle four times on the stain. "Pretty impressive." Jonathan looked at the camera, holding the bottle with both hands. "Gentle Koala Cleaning Spray. Getting rid of stains," he pulled the trigger again, "is just a spray away."

"Cut! Better!" Spencer's voice called.

Blaine walked over. "I like the track you're on. Keep going with it."

"Are you sure?"

"Yes, remember: just get into the moment. Life is comprised of moments, one after another. If you can enter into this moment, then you are fully alive."

"Got it!"

Jonathan Celestial looked at the orange bottle, nearly depleted by him. He held it in his hands, hoping that it might whisper to him what to say. It was silent.

"You know," Spencer began, "I can write down some ideas for lines if you like. We want this thing to be thirty seconds max."

Blaine said, "That would be—"

"No," Jonathan answered, "this is going to be the perfect take. Right here, right now."

"Okay, buddy," Spencer was wiping his glasses.

Once more the camera was rolling.

Jonathan pointed at the pants. "Do you have tough stains to get rid of?" He lifted up the bottle. "Give Gentle Koala Cleaning Spray a chance. It works well to take out even the most stubborn stain." He sprayed it on the pants, pulling the trigger only a couple times. "See how it works? Stain all gone." Jonathan turned to face the camera. "Gentle Koala Cleaning Spray: gentle on skin, tough on stains."

"Cut! That's the one! That's it!"

Spencer ran over and patted Jonathan on the shoulder. "Great work, kid. You're a natural at this. Where did you come up with that line about gentleness? That was freaking brilliant!"

"I have my sources," Jonathan stammered.

"Nice job," Blaine said. "See? When you enter into the moment, great things can happen."

They walked out of the studio and down the street.

"You sure did a number on that commercial," Blaine said, walking slowly. "I think you could be pretty good at acting."

Jonathan's eyes brightened. "Really?!"

"Yes, you just need…a little more focus. That's all."

They had dinner together, and that night, laying down on a futon, Jonathan opened up his book:

Jobs, occupations, and vocations are of profound importance to humans. For some, they possess the capacity to bring about existential fulfillment. For others, they are simply a means to survive. Finding one's calling, as humans put it, is of great significance. The search for it can be difficult, and may last even a lifetime, but it is a noble endeavor indeed. Only when the search for fulfillment in work supersedes all else, we stars observe, does it become a problem. How can a human achieve harmony with his or her job?

Standing in the doorway was Blaine. He was smiling. "That check you got is pretty nice."

"Is it?"

Blaine nodded and entered walked towards the futon where Jonathan was reclining.

"You know, I don't like most people. However, I don't mind you, Jonathan. I suppose I can let you stay one more night."

"Another night?"

"Sure." Still smiling, he turned off the light switch and said goodnight.

"After all," Blaine said, "you're the star of the show. Who doesn't like to have a star around?"

Day 5

Waking up to sunlit rain, Jonathan realized he was alone in the apartment named *Eclipse*.

He yawned, and feeling he wanted to sleep longer, got back into bed. However, he was unable to sleep.

"What if he finds out?" he wondered aloud.

Rising from the bed, he went into the common area, which was spotlessly clean. He sat on the couch, and watched the rain fall. At that moment, he noticed that there was a piece of paper on the table. He walked over, picked it up, and read it:

Jonathan,

At work.
The café is called Java city. It's on 45th and Densmore.
Feel free to visit.
Don't make any stains on the carpet. We don't have Gentle Koala.

-Blaine

Smirking, he put down the paper, and went back to the window. He looked out at the view of the city. In the distance was a park, which Blaine identified as Gasworks Park last night. Jonathan thought it might be nice to go there sometime.

He put on a coat, which made him feel the most like a star as he had in the last few days, and stepped outside.

Up 45th he walked. He passed café after café, each filled with people enjoying coffee. None of these venues was Java City. There was an arts and crafts store, a church, a donut store, several restaurants, and a bar full of pinball machines. At the bar he looked through a window and saw the flashing colors, which reminded him of a display of stars.

Continuing to make his way, he felt the rain fall on him. He embraced it. Joy once more returned to him. He was on a vacation of sorts, searching for something, just glad to be away from space. Looking up at the tapestry of clouds intermingling with Comrade Sun, his jaw lowered and his eyes grew big. He felt his arm, and realized that there were little bumps on it. There was something about that feeling that was perfect.

A sign hanging overhead revealed the café Jonathan was seeking. Just outside the door to the café was a news dispenser, which had papers in it. These papers, Jonathan surmised, held the secrets to what was going on everywhere else in the world. This particular newspaper was free. Jonathan reached in to pick it up and was surprised to see that the most pressing piece of news was not somewhere far away like London; it was in Seattle:

Massive, Mysterious Crater in Volunteer Park Beguiles and Horrifies

Passing through the doorway of the café, Jonathan crossed paths with a man in a trench coat who had blonde hair and a cold expression.

"Excuse me," the man said.

"You are excused."

The man turned and scrutinized Jonathan carefully. He looked at him for several seconds. "Quite."

Jonathan paused, and then cried, "Have a great day!"

The man watched Jonathan as he left the café.

Turning his head one way and then another, Jonathan opened the door of the café and entered. He was greeted by a rush of warm air and the smell of croissants. Approaching the cash register, he saw Blaine standing behind a machine that made whirring and steaming sounds.

In Blaine's hand was a small spoon of sorts, full of a coffee that was ground up. He put the spoon into the machine, and a fine liquid poured into the small glasses beneath. Silky smooth, almost like velvet, this must have been espresso in its purest form. Blaine continued to watch the espresso pour, and then he transferred it into a tiny cup, which he put on the counter for a young girl to retrieve. She took the cup of coffee, and then went to sit with another girl. This other girl had blonde hair and brown eyes. She was engrossed in reading. The two girls sat together. As the girl with pure espresso enjoyed her drink, so too did the girl who was reading take sip after sip from a tall cup of coffee. Jonathan watched all of this, not thinking much of it.

At the counter, a bespectacled youngster asked, "What can I get started for you?"

Jonathan looked at Blaine, who faintly smiled, then at the girls, and then back at the cashier, saying, "I want coffee!"

"Sure thing, boss."

Excited, Jonathan walked over to Blaine and stood on the other side of the counter.

"So this is your job?" Jonathan asked.

"You got it. We all gotta work. Most of us, at least."

"It's a nice café! The air is permeated with the scent of coffee."

"Yeah, well, that's what we serve here, if you could believe it."

Blaine slid another drink onto the counter. Jonathan reached for it.

"Whoa, there. That's for someone else."

Blaine turned around. When he reappeared he had a cup of coffee in his hand. "This is yours," he said.

Jonathan immediately drank all the coffee. "How late do you work?" he asked.

"Until 3." Blaine looked at Jonathan's feet and then met his eyes. "You gonna stand there until then?"

"No."

"Well, you can have a seat with those two girls over there, if you're feeling brave. They're both friends of mine. The one on the left is Janelle, and the one reading is Lyla."

"Lyla?"

"You got it."

Jonathan looked around the café, rolled up his sleeves, and said, "I think I will have a seat with them."

"Feel free. I'm here 'til 3."

Making his way over to the two girls, Jonathan remembered the etiquette and manners from his studies.

"Pardon me, ladies. Would it be an affront if I sat here?"

The two girls looked at each and smiled.

"Sure thing!" Janelle exclaimed.

Jonathan sat directly across from Lyla.

There was a pause. Jonathan said, "It is a nice day, is it not? I am referring to the weather."

Lyla looked up from her book. "What do you want?" she asked.

Sweat forming in his brow, Jonathan replied, "What I want is to enjoy my day. What do YOU want?"

Lyla turned a page. "For you to go away. I'm trying to enjoy my book."

Jonathan was rising from his chair when Janelle said, "It's okay! You can stay here. Don't mind my friend. She can be a little…I don't know."

"Honest?" Lyla said.

"What did I do, anyway?" Jonathan asked. He crossed his arms.

But Lyla didn't speak; she kept reading.

Jonathan leaned back in his chair and asked, "How… how do you know Blaine?"

"College," Janelle answered. "We were in a lot of history classes together."

"I see." Jonathan was nodding.

"How do you know Blaine?" Janelle asked, pointing at Jonathan.

"I…met him at a concert."

"Oh, cool!"

"Do you like Static Sea?"

"Static Sea is great!" Janelle beamed. "They're playing a show this Tuesday."

"I love Static Sea!" Jonathan nearly shouted. "They are my favorite band."

"Good for you…" Lyla mumbled.

Another pause followed. Janelle put down her finished beverage and asked, "You going to the party tomorrow night?"

"I didn't know I was invited. Who is hosting?"

"Your friend Blaine the rock star is hosting."

Jonathan turned to face Blaine, who was making a drink.

"Hey, Blaine."

"Yes, Jonathan?"

"Can I come to your party tomorrow night?"

"Little busy right now, buddy. Gonna have to think about what you're saying later."

"Please?"

"Two shots…three pumps…"

"Please?"

Lyla was giggling. Her laugh was high-pitched and had a nasal quality. She put down her book and looked at Jonathan.

Jonathan continued:

"Blaine—"

"You know what? I guess you can go to the party. I suppose I'll allow it. That okay, girls?"

"Sure!" Janelle said with cheer.

"No way," Lyla replied.

"Well it's too late." Blaine gestured with an arm. "I hereby invite thee to attend my festival."

"Awesome!" Jonathan cheered.

"Consider me uninvited," Lyla said.

Jonathan rose from the table. "Well, I suppose I will see the two of you, or at least one of you, tomorrow night. Where is the festival?"

"It's a party, Jonathan," Blaine said.

"Oh, well where is the party?"

"At our apartment."

"'Our apartment'?!" the girls said in unison.

"No, no, no. I mean. Um." Blaine wiped his forehead. "What I meant to say was that the party will be held at the apartment. The. It's an article, and a determinator."

Jonathan was smiling a big grin.

The two girls laughed. Janelle said, "We should probably get going, but it has been really nice to meet you, Jonathan. What's your last name?"

"Celestial."

"Well, aren't you a special one," Lyla chided.

"Hey! I am special," Jonathan said, crossing his arms against his chest.

With that, the two girls were gone.

Jonathan ordered another coffee and continued to sit at the table.

"Blaine?"

"Yes, Jonathan?"

"What time is it?"

"Time for you to go out and get some fresh air."

"But what time is it?"

"12:30."

Jonathan got up, said goodbye, and left he café. He walked down the street.

Hey, Sun.

Hi Jonathan! How's your vacation?

Not bad.

Making any progress on your search for…what was it?

You know what. It will come to you.

Oh yeah, that's right! I remember now. Anyway, how's that going?

I don't know. But tomorrow, I'm going to a party. How neat is that?

That's pretty incredible Jonathan. I'm proud of you. You know, I look forward to seeing you when your PTO is exhausted.

Um…yeah, me too.

Anyway, I gotta go. Cloud coverage.

Understood.

Shine on ya later!

Later.

Walking down the hill along 45th street, thinking about coffee, meeting new people, and sharing an apartment, Jonathan sighed. "Going back…to being a star. Right."

He took a turn and entered Gasworks Park. A nearby slope of bright-green grass was inviting to him, so he made his way up the winding path towards the top. Standing on top of the hill, he beheld the city once more, this time from a different view. There was water and tall buildings, hills on both sides of Downtown. Planes flew overhead; boats sailing along the smooth choppy water.

Suddenly, he remembered what happened all those millions of years ago. In the same instance, it felt like a lifetime ago, and yet it was planted in his consciousness so vividly, as though he was reliving it right now. He felt the heart in his chest pump wildly. It felt like something terrible was about to happen at any moment. He raised his hands to touch his temple. He opened his mouth to scream but didn't. He fell to the ground and remained there.

After a couple of minutes he felt his heart slow back down. He stood back up on his feet. He looked at the city. He lifted both his hands and cupped the view of the buildings in them. He ran down the winding path of the slope until he was at the entrance of the park. It started to rain again. He walked all the way back to *Eclipse*. He went inside, got onto the futon, and felt his head whirl with thoughts.

Day 6

It was common knowledge, the tale of how stars came to dominate the universe with their light.

Jonathan recalled the history clearly. Long ago, before what anyone could remember, and even before that, there was the great shadow. Oppressive, overwhelming, the great shadow was like a void, a nothingness that extended infinitely. One day, a celestial being named Sir Cosmsos was traveling through this great shadow, bemoaning his inability to do anything or see. Nobody knows for sure who or what created Sir Cosmsos, but he existed nonetheless.

Wearing a stylish hat, Sir Cosmos wandered, that is, until he collided with another celestial being who was named the Star Keeper. No more than a second-rate scientist with a white coat at that time, the Star Keeper had a question: What, the Star Keeper wondered, if the denser, colder regions of molecular clouds collapsed on themselves? What would happen then? Sir Cosmos, who knew little of such things, hadn't the faintest idea what would result, but he knew that the Star Keeper was on to something.

The two of them decided that it would be good to partner up. So the Star Keeper traveled throughout the great shadow, creating molecular clouds, and then watching as stars began to form. Slowly but surely, the universe became a little less shadowy, and a little less dark. Over the course of billions of years, the stars grew and developed, and Sir Cosmos delegated the Star Keeper to be the supervisor, overseeing their work as they lit up the universe. Sir Cosmos, it was decided, would be the Star

Keepers own boss, and be the leader of all the celestial beings.

This is the story Jonathan Celestial was born into. For a billion years, he worked hard, lighting up his sphere of a galaxy.

Then something happened that changed everything for Jonathan. No longer was there any going back.

Jonathan Celestial thought of all of this as he walked with Blaine back to *Eclipse*. On his mind was one question. It was a question that popped into his brain every now and then:

Who created Sir Cosmos?

Meanwhile, Blaine was speaking:

"You can stay a bit longer, at least until we get you back on your feet."

"But I'm already on my feet. I'm walking!"

"Literally, you are the most literal person I've ever met. Come on; we got a party to attend."

Inside, there was soft, gentle, ambient rock music playing, not unlike the sounds of Static Sea. People were standing around chatting, drinking out of red cups. There were Christmas lights hanging from the ceiling, and the door to the outer deck was open.

"You know," Blaine said while picking up a red cup. "In about a week we'll be filming a music video for the lead single on our new album. Might you like to be in it, Mr. Actor?"

Seated on the couch, Jonathan turned to look at Blaine and said, "I'd love to!"

"Okay, cool. We can discuss my creative vision later."

"Sounds good."

"If you're lucky, I might even let you play the lead role."

"Really?"

Blaine sipped his drink. "After that heartfelt performance in the Koala commercial? Of course I'd consider it."

Jonathan turned his head to look at the others seated on the couch. There was a fellow who wore a backwards baseball cap. He had a pen in his ear.

Reaching out a hand, Jonathan said, "I'm Jonathan Celestial. How are you?"

The guy with the cap looked startled. "Jonathan Celestial? That has a nice ring to it. It is giving me an idea." He reached into his back pocket, pulled out a small note pad, and proceeded to write in it."

"What are you writing?"

The guy looked up. "Oh, nothing. Nothing. Just getting some thoughts down."

"What about? What's your name?"

The guy turned his cap around, and then rotated it back to how it had been seconds before. "My name is Rob. Sorry for not telling you sooner."

"Not a problem."

"So what do you do, Mr. Celestial?"

"I'm…I'm an actor?"

"Oh yeah? What have you been in?"

Jonathan looked at his hand for a moment, then at Rob. "I was in a commercial for Gentle Koala Cleaning Spray."

"Right on."

There was a pause. Jonathan was still adjusting to the flow of human conversation.

"What do you do?" he asked Rob.

Still writing in his note pad, Rob looked up and said, "I film and do design work on the side."

"What do you design?"

"Depends on the project. Mostly digital."

"How do you know Blaine?"

Rob put down the note pad. "Me? I film his stuff."

Blaine turned to look at the two of them:

"I was just telling Jonathan about the music video. That's super funny."

Jonathan looked around. "But nobody's laughing…"

Rob held the pen to his chin. It appeared as though he was staring through Jonathan.

"What's wrong?" Jonathan asked Rob.

"Oh, nothing. Nothing at all. I'm just thinking about the opening shot."

Jonathan turned to Blaine. "What's the creative vision for the music video?" he asked.

Blaine was grinning as he set down his red cup. "You heard the man. Tell him the vision, Rob."

Rob crossed his left leg over his right. "What we want to go for with this music video is the theme of growth. What I am picturing is a gardener who sows seeds in a field. Throughout the video, the seeds turn into flowers, which bloom in a magnificent display. At the end, a boy picks a flower and offers it to a girl."

"I see," Jonathan replied. "How old is the boy?"

"How old are you?" Blaine yelled.

"Twenty-five."

"Well, then the boy is twenty-five."

Jonathan sighed. "It's an interesting idea. I'd be happy to contribute."

"Or you can be a flower," Blaine continued. "Maybe a pansy."

"A what?"

"Or you can be the girl. The choice is yours."

Rob turned uncrossed his legs, and then crossed his right leg over his left. "The theme of growth is timeless. The gardener, of course, represents God. The flowers are his people. When the flower gets plucked…"

But Jonathan was thinking of something else entirely. In his human studies courses, he learned about God and organized religion. Wanting to check something, he said, "Excuse me for just one moment," and rose from the couch.

Inside the spare room, which Blaine said Jonathan could temporarily call his own, a guy was pouring a bottle of something into his red cup. Ignoring him, Jonathan opened up On Humanity and turned to the section on God. He read:

> *Theoretically, there are as many conceptions, as many understandings of "God" as there are sentient beings. Some consider there to only be one God, while others think there are thousands. Some think there is no God. There is no consensus. While organized, structured religions seek the truth of knowing a transcendent reality, others worship and practice spirituality through more individual ways. Regardless, most stories of religion and spirituality attempt to make sense of creation, that is, how stars and celestial bodies could grow from nothing to the present reality.*

Jonathan walked back to the couch. Rob didn't look up from the writing he was doing until Jonathan waved a hand in his face.

"I'm back," he said.

"Hey. So yeah, as I was saying, the gardener is God, and —"

"Hey, Blaine," Jonathan said.

"What is it, Jonathan?"

"Do you believe that there is a God."

"No way."

"Okay."

Blaine grabbed another red cup and stacked it on the first. "Why, do you?"

Jonathan paused. "I don't know."

Rob put down his notebook. Jonathan could see the etchings inside, which were impossible to read.

Rob leaned towards Jonathan. "The thing about there being a God is—"

"Why you getting all cerebral?" Blaine asked. "You're at a party."

"Sorry." Rob looked embarrassed.

Jonathan said, "I think your idea for the music video is interesting. I'd be happy to play the part of the boy."

What Jonathan was wondering was whether it was possible that God created Sir Cosmos. However, he felt that there was no way to know for sure, at least not yet. But, at the same time, it seemed to him that this path of thinking was leading him towards something substantial. What he needed was a chance to think.

Rob said, "We haven't decided the ending, though."

"You mean after the boy gives the girl the flower?"

Rob nodded and held the bill of his hat. "Blaine and I —"

"We can't decide if the girl will accept the flower and fall in love with you or not. Depends on how charming you can be, I suppose."

Jonathan said, "I can be charming."

Blaine laughed.

Rob picked up his notebook and leafed through it, searching for something.

"Who's going to play the girl?" Jonathan asked, wondering if he was talking to himself.

Blaine answered, "Not sure. Know any girls?"

"There were two friends of yours at the café yesterday."

"No there weren't."

"Lyla and Janelle."

"Nope."

Rob said, "I think Janelle could play the part pretty well. Anyway, what I'm struggling with is calculating the pacing for the video. "#43" is eight minutes long, so that gives us—"

"A whole lot of shots of flowers blooming," Blaine added.

Jonathan, who had no interest in alcohol, excused himself and went to the coffee machine, which Blain taught him to use the other day.

At that moment there was the sound of voices getting louder. Jonathan looked away from the coffee machine to see that Janelle was now present at the party. Jonathan walked over:

"How's it going?"

"Great! Wonderful!"

Relieved, Jonathan asked, "Where's Lyla?"

"Oh, she isn't really the party type. She can be awfully shy, you know."

"There's the beautiful maiden for the music video!" Blaine exclaimed, stacking another red cup.

She gave no attention to Blaine, but stood by Jonathan.

"Are you gonna be involved in the music video?"

"He's gonna be the sun," Blaine said.

Rob put down his pen. "Well, I didn't think we were going to personify the sun that much, were we?"

Janelle looked at the stacked cups next to Blaine. "Looks like someone just came to their first party."

"Good one!"

Jonathan heard the sound of the coffee machine beeping. He grabbed a mug that had a Static Sea sticker on it and poured himself some.

Jonathan turned to Janelle. "Well, if you see Lyla, tell her I said hi."

"Sure thing!"

Jonathan didn't like Lyla and her unkind attitude, but he felt sorry that she didn't want to go to the party. He stepped out of the common room and back into his own room. He opened his book and then closed it again. He didn't know what to make of things. He turned to gaze at a calendar that was pinned on the wall. The picture depicted a deer in the forest. Jonathan started to count how many days he spent as a human. It was tempting to think about what he accomplished so far.

He sighed and let his arms hang at his side.

He walked to the window and looked to see where the Moon was, but he decided he didn't want to talk to him.

Not wanting to be out in the party atmosphere, which was getting louder and more insipid by the second, he got into the bed that Blaine made for him, tossed and turned, and eventually fell asleep.

Day 7

Jonathan Celestial and Blaine were walking along the shore in Golden Gardens Park on a drizzly June day.

"Amazing! Awesome! Astonishing!" Jonathan exclaimed, pointing at Puget Sound, that vast body of water between the city and the mountains.

Blaine replied, "I thought I remember you saying you were from here."

"Doesn't mean I can't be astounded by the beauty that is afforded me."

"Fair enough."

Blaine leaned down, picked up a rock, and hurled it into the sea. It skipped twice before sinking below.

"That's pretty good," Jonathan said. He picked up a stone of his own. His hand, supercharged with gravitational energy, launched the rock into the water, where it skipped seventeen times before disappearing from view.

"How did you—"

"Oops. I mean, I do this a lot."

Blaine looked at Jonathan with an incredulous expression. "You know," he said, "you have a knack for surprising me. Seriously. You keep surprising me every day that I know you."

"Oh, I didn't mean to…I'm sorry."

"No, don't be sorry. It's great. I love it."

They continued walking. "That Rob guy seemed like a thoughtful, interesting fellow," Jonathan said.

"Yes, well, he is eccentric?"

"Is he?"

"You talked to him. What do you think?"

"Well, he was rather on the…eclectic side."

"Now we're just splitting semantic hairs. Anyway, he is a FANTASTIC cameraman. He has done all the work for Static Sea."

Jonathan picked up another rock and then dropped it. "Cool."

"He'll be going with us on the trip."

Jonathan stopped. "What trip?"

"Oh, we're going camping in a few days. Just for a night. We're going to Cool Waters State Park."

"I hope the water isn't too cold!"

Blaine raised an eyebrow. "It's just a name."

"Who else is going on the trip?"

Blaine trotted up towards a log and jumped on it. He walked along it like a trapeze artist. "It's sort of a guys' night out. There'll be me, Tim, Mitch, Rob, and you, if you aren't too busy starring in cleaning spray commercials."

"Don't worry; I won't be."

Blaine was looking at his feet as he walked. "Good."

"You said I could stay with you until I was standing up. So—"

"No. I said you could stay until you were back on your feet. You've almost burned through the money from that commercial, so we need to think of something else for you to do."

"But what?"

Blaine took a few steps in front of Jonathan. "Not sure. Maybe we could film a movie in which a hero has to skip rocks to save the world. You seem to be pretty great at that."

Jonathan nodded. "I could do that."

"But in all seriousness, I think some time communing with the natural world would really benefit us all. It could help the band bond before the series of shows."

Jonathan caught up to him, and the two of them stood still, gazing out at the water. Then Jonathan sprinted towards the sea. With a series of splashes he was up to his knees in water. Never before had he experienced something so invigorating, so full of life. It gave Jonathan a sense of fantastic ecstasy.

"What in the—"

Jonathan was laughing, splashing the water with his hands. The tide was gentle and merciful towards the plaid shirt Blaine loaned him. He turned around to look at Blaine, as though inviting him in. Then, with no thinking, he submerged his head in the water. Cold, marine bliss followed as he tasted the salty water. He lifted his head up and splashed water, little droplets flying into the air.

Shaking and clutching himself followed.

They walked back, away from the water, back up the sloping sands towards Blaine's car.

"Like I said earlier," Blaine said. "You keep on surprising me."

Blaine threw a blanket at Jonathan, who continued to shiver while wearing it. They stood outside of Blaine's car for several minutes.

"Once you're dry, we can get in and I'll crank the heat."

It started to rain. As though Jonathan hadn't encountered enough water already, here it was, falling from the heavens, landing on his head, in his hands, on his feet. He laughed.

"Okay, we can go—"

"Excuse me, you two."

Blaine and Jonathan turned to see a man who looked familiar to Jonathan, though he couldn't recall from where. It was not as though he had met that many people in his life.

The man had blonde hair and cold, blue eyes. He pulled out a badge, waved it in the air, and then said, "My name is Agent Gray Willows. I am with the Bureau for Astral Anomalies." He pointed at Jonathan with a slender finger. "You. I'd like to talk to you privately, if that is all right with you. If it is not all right with you…well, that might seem suspicious, now wouldn't it?"

Jonathan looked at Blaine, and then at the Agent. "Sure, we can talk."

The two of them walked twenty steps away from the car, to the edge of the parking lot.

Gray Willows said, "I should explain some things. At present, I am in the middle of an investigation concerning a large crater that was formed in Volunteer Park. The moment I saw you I recognized you." He turned to directly face Jonathan. "I believe I ran into you at the entrance of a certain café. Moreover, I saw you walking through the park, right by the crater, the day it was formed."

"Okay."

"So," the Agent continued, "I would like to have you come to my office for questioning, just so I can understand things a bit better." His eyes looked even colder. "Would that be acceptable to you?"

Jonathan knew he had to go. If he didn't it would appear suspicious. All he wanted in that moment was to be speeding away in Blaine's car, the heat at full blast. Instead, he was shivering in a parking lot, talking to this guy.

"Sure, I'll go."

Willows smiled, his teeth crooked and sharp. "Wonderful. Are you available tomorrow at noon?"

"Yes, I am."

"Outstanding." Willows patted Jonathan on the shoulder, which didn't feel right. "Here's my card. I will see you at my office downtown. I will see you then."

Jonathan gazed down at the flip flops he was wearing. When he looked back up, the Agent was gone.

"Where did he…"

Blaine ran up to Jonathan. "You okay?" he asked.

Jonathan was shivering, desperate to be warm. Then he realized something. Concentrating, closing his eyes, he emanated thermal energy, and in an instant he was completely dry.

Blaine took a step back. "You're freaking me out!"

"Sorry."

"No, it's fine. Just don't do anything else wacky. Seriously."

"I won't. I promise!"

They made their way back to the car. "What did that Agent guy want, anyway?"

Jonathan informed him of his appointment the next day.

"Interesting. I remember we had a show at Volunteer Park that day. That was where I first met you. I thought you were some freak. In fact, I still think you're some freak."

"Thanks, Blaine. I appreciate that."

"Any time. Listen, you gotta tell me what you're gonna say to him at the interview tomorrow."

They got into the car and pulled out of the lot. The clouds above were steadfast, the rain continuing to fall.

Jonathan tipped his seat back. "What am I going to tell him? That I incidentally walked by a crater."

"How did you 'incidentally' walk by a crater?"

Jonathan swallowed. "I don't' know. I guess I just didn't really notice it."

"How could you not notice it?"

"I don't know. I just didn't."

"How are you feeling about the interview?" Blaine slammed the breaks to meet a stop sign.

Jonathan was nervous. He could always return to working as a star. But he never wanted to go back there. On the other hand, if he remained a human and was imprisoned for having destroyed public property, then his PTO would be used up in no time. Either way, he knew he would become a star again, which brought him feelings of dread. So, if he was going to be a star again, he needed to find something of lasting meaning, something significant to bring back with him. This investigation could completely compromise that search.

"I don't know how I feel," he finally answered.

"Did you do anything wrong?"

"No."

"Then you should be fine, right? Nothing to fear."

"Yes, but what if they think I did something wrong, and I get put in a jail cell?" His voice was shaking.

"Then I will be the one who moves in with you." Blaine was smiling.

"I don't feel great about it. That guy, the Agent, he had a peculiar way about him. Something felt...off about him."

Blaine looked at Jonathan and said, "I can see why you might feel that way. But really, you should be fine. We can rehearse some answers to questions later. We can pin down your story so that you shine in the interview."

"Thanks, Blaine."

"Of course."

Half an hour later they returned to the apartment. After dinner, and the rehearsing of his story, Jonathan went to his room and tried to sleep. But rest was far away. Tossing, turning, he eventually got up, walked into the common area, which was immaculately clean, and then slid open the sliding door to step out on the balcony.

Only a few celestial bodies would have a significant conversation with Jonathan. One of those beings was the Moon. Knowing what to expect, but feeling lonely and desiring a celestial companion, Jonathan closed his eyes and called out:

Hello?

There was no response. He tried again:

Hello?

What?

Hi, Moon.

Oh, Jonathan.

How are you?

Does it matter? It's another beautiful night, but one day, we're all going to be gone.

I suppose that's true. But still, it is beautiful, isn't it?

I guess.

I'm having a tough time with this human business. You see, I am —

Well why are you bothering me with your story? What could I possibly even do to help you, anyway?

I just wanted to share, Moon.

Fine then. Don't expect me to work any miracles.

Anyway, I'm having a tough time. I'm trying to find purpose, to find some healing, but—

Healing is always a long ways off, Jonathan.

So it would seem. I've been down here for…for a whole week, and I feel like I'm not figuring anything out. Well, I did have a lot of fun playing in the water today. You know, you really do a great job regulating the tides, Moon.

Sure I do. Anyone could do my job. I'm surprised I still have it.

But I just don't know what to do, Moon. This Agent from some governmental investigation wants to talk to me.

I wish someone would talk to me.

Moon, I'm talking to you right now.

So?

Never mind. The point is, I'm afraid this Agent fellow is going to prevent me from my search, and that I'm going to return to being a star again.

Well of course you're going to return to being a star again. And a few billion years later, you'll be a white dwarf, just a bright mass of death.

That's not exactly the perspective I was going for. Do you have any advice for me?

Advice?

Yes, any words of wisdom. I know you're wise, even if you don't think so.

Just remember that none of it really matters. That's the truth. Everything ends.

Thanks, Moon. Thanks a lot.

You asked for it.

I think I need to go.

Everyone who talks to me always wants to go.

I'm really sorry. I'll talk to you again soon.

Sure you will. You know, it's awfully lonesome here in the night sky. So much space.

I'll talk to you soon, Moon.

Okay, Jonathan.

With that, Jonathan climbed into the bed, turned off the light, and tossed and turned all night.

Day 8

Waking up to a ringing phone was not what Jonathan Celestial preferred, but such was his reality as he opened his eyes.

He picked up the phone. It continued to ring. He talked into it, only to realize that he needed to press the green button to actually hear who was calling speak:

"Hello?"

"Yes, hello. Is this Jonathan Celestial?"

"It is."

"Hello, Jonathan. My name is Bernice. I am calling from the office of Mr. Gray Willows. How are you doing today?"

"Fine."

"So good to hear. Jonathan, I am afraid to inform you that your appointment with Mr. Willows will need to be rescheduled. You see, he has an urgent matter to attend to today, one he did not anticipate. If possible, he would like to meet with you tomorrow at 1:00pm Would that be acceptable to you?"

"Um, sure."

"Wonderful. Well, we will see you then."

"Okay. Thanks."

"And Jonathan…"

"Yes?"

"Please do be sure to be on time. Mr. Willows is a punctual man. So, please respect his time."

"Sure thing."

"Thanks"

"Thank you, Jonathan."

He put the phone down. He rose from the bed, walked over to the window, and looked out at the neighborhood below. Students were walking towards the University campus. While some students had hands in their pockets and earbuds in, others walked in groups, talking loudly and occasionally laughing. Jonathan watched the students, envying their innocence, and then went to prepare for the day.

First, he made coffee. When the machine beeped, he clapped his hands with delight and poured himself a cup. After a quick shower and a bowl of cereal he grabbed his book, walked down the stairs, and left *Eclipse*.

It was a cool day, Comrade Sun occasionally poking through the clouds. Jonathan sighed. He was sure to look both ways before crossing the street. Up a hill he went, and then he was on the campus.

Red Square was an expanse of brick, with students and professors walking every which way. In the distance was an old building that had colorful windows. Jonathan knew this was the library.

Inside, he was pleased by the quiet calm that filled the air. He walked through the entryway with a straight, almost robotic posture, his gait neutral. The sound of a page turning could be heard, along with whispers and fingers typing on computers. Passing one stack and then another, Jonathan approached a table, sat down, and opened his book:

> *Though humans value education, it has become institutionalized so that knowledge and truth have become divorced from character development and other things that contribute to a more holistic, complete individual. Vocation, spirituality, political engagement, the aforementioned character development, have all become compartmentalized to the point that it is difficult to connect them. Furthermore, cost and other barriers prevent many humans from attaining their highest level of education, causing an elitism to persist.*

"What are you doing here?"

Seated across from him, arms crossed, was Lyla.

"I um, I was just looking for a place to read."

"Can't you go somewhere else?"

Turning to look directly into Lyla's eyes, Jonathan said, "I, well, I have every right to be here as you."

"I know. It's fine. I don't care if you're here."

"It sure is a nice library—"

"Did you hear me? I said I don't care."

"Okay, fine."

"What are you reading?"

Jonathan answered, "It's a book I'm reading."

"I can see that, weirdo. What's it called?"

Jonathan turned the spine of the book towards her, anxious that his starhood would be found out.

Lyla put a piece of gum in her mouth and chewed it. "Humanity huh. Sounds boring."

"It's actually really fascinating."

"I'm sure it is. You're a human, reading about humans. So riveting."

Jonathan stood up from the table. "Look, I don't know what your issue with me is, but I'd like to know. I really would."

Lyla sat down at the table and folded her hands on it. She smiled. "You know, there's just something about you that makes me want to mess with you. I can't explain it."

"Well, I'd appreciate it if you didn't."

Lyla yawned. "Thank you for your request. It will be addressed in the order it was received."

Jonathan, not expecting a sincere answer but curious nonetheless, asked, "So what did you study?"

"Me?"

"Yes, you."

Lyla lifted her left hand up into the air, gesturing. "I am doing a graduate degree on the cosmos. I am studying Astronomy."

Jonathan smiled. "Really?"

"Yes. To be honest, I am fascinated with space. Always have been. When I was a little girl, we lived out in the country, and I would run out into a field and look up at the night sky. Draco. Aquila. The Big Dipper. I loved finding constellations and all that good stuff." She looked directly at Jonathan, her blue eyes big. "But what do you know about any of that?"

"Me? Nothing. I know nothing about stars. I don't even know what a star is."

"That's what I thought, Mr. Humanity. Anyway, when I graduated, I ended up in my current job, which is awful and stupid."

"What…what do you do?"

She sighed. "I'm a receptionist at a dental clinic."

"Well, I bet you just brighten the days of everyone you see." He smirked as he said this.

"Not as bright as the number Dr. Robinson DDS does on their teeth, though."

"Of course not. We all have our limits."

She smiled. For the first time, Jonathan saw her genuinely smile. "You're such a weirdo," she said.

"What can I be but my true self?"

"A liar? A fake?"

"I suppose so."

Again she folded her hands. "I met Blaine in college. I was really impressed by Static Sea. You know how everyone has a friend whose in a band, and how they pretend to like their music, but it's really just because they know them? It's not like that with Static Sea. I actually really like their music."

"Good for you."

"Good for me. What did you study?"

Jonathan thought about how to answer. "Philosophy."

She raised her hands in the air, gesturing dramatically. "Truth, thy nature eludes me."

"Indeed."

"Makes sense, though. Explains the book you're reading, which would give the Russian greats a run for their money."

"Sure would."

"So, then, Mr. Weirdo Humanity. What is your philosophy? Tell me."

Jonathan cleared his throat. "To tell you the truth, I'm still figuring that out."

"Safe answer. Of course you are."

"I am searching for something, to be honest."

"And what is that?"

Jonathan looked once more into her eyes as he spoke:

"I'm looking for truth, for purpose, for hope."

Lyla leaned back in her chair. "That is just the most precious thing I did ever hear. Beautiful!" she said in an over-dramatic voice.

Jonathan stammered. "You asked. That's what I'm looking for."

Lyla pointed at the ceiling. "Are you expecting to find hope, here, in the library?"

"Why not? I suppose I have a lot to learn from this book."

"Maybe you should focus on living, and not on thinking about living."

Jonathan put a hand through his hair. "But if a person doesn't think about how they live, then all they do is wander aimlessly. If I'm going to find what I'm looking for, I need to know what to be keeping an eye out for."

"I guess that makes sense."

Jonathan rose from his seat and walked towards the exit of the library. "I need to go," he said.

"Don't be gone long."

Outside, Jonathan tried to reach The Sun:
You there?

Hi Jonathan! I'm here, but only for a moment. It's so hard to shine here, what with all these clouds.

Sun, I'm having a tough time. Tell me, what am I looking for? What am I hoping to gain from being down here?

Jonathan, no need to despair. Um, well, you mentioned you were looking for something to reinvigorate yourself, to bring back that nuclear fusion, so to speak , so I should think that you are looking for something good, yes?

'Something good'? Yes, Sun, I'm looking for something good! But what? I just don't know. I'm wandering in the dark.

No you're not, Jonathan. You got me to light things up for you! Remember: no matter how cloudy it is, I'm always shining. Even if you can't see me, I'm shining.

Thanks, Sun.

Now, I need to get going; clouds are coming. Later, Jonathan!

Bye.

Confused, afraid, Jonathan walked through the university campus quickly, full of dread.

Day 9

Jonathan Celestial and Blaine arrived in front of the tall, menacing building where Agent Gray Willows worked. In Jonathan's hand he held a leather wallet that contained nothing except a fake ID and money for the bus.

"All right," Blaine said. "You're gonna be fine. Just stick to the script, okay?'

"Okay."

In the waiting room, Jonathan saw a pile of old magazines. He reached towards one that depicted a leopard in the wild.

"Jonathan?" a voice called.

He rose. A woman was standing at the entrance of the hallway.

She reached out a hand. He shook it, and noticed that it felt cold.

"Hello, Jonathan. I'm Bernice. We spoke on the phone."

"Yes, I remember."

"If you will follow me, I will take you to Mr. Willows."

"Hello, Mr. Celestial. How are you?" Agent Gray reached out a hand to shake. His grip was firm and his hand was cold like Bernice's.

"Swell, I am swell," Jonathan replied.

Behind two large doors was the Agent's office. Outside the windows was a panoramic view of downtown, the buildings majestic and awe-instilling.

"Please, have a seat."

Jonathan sat in a big, comfortable chair, and looked straight into the eyes of Agent Gray. What he saw were two small, blue eyes that emanated coldness just like his handshake. Jonathan knew he had to pass the interview if he was going to continue his search.

"May I see identification?" Agent Gray asked.

"Yes, identification, yes." Jonathan reached into a pocket and pulled out his wallet. He handed it to the Agent.

Agent Gray took the ID card out of the wallet. "Jonathan Celestial. A nice name indeed."

Jonathan bowed his head in polite deference.

Leaning back in his chair, the Agent said, "So tell me about what you were doing at Volunteer Park, right by where that hideous crater formed."

"Well, I, I was going for a walk through the park to the café…"

"Oh?"

"Yes, it is my favorite park to walk through."

"I see. When did you notice the crater?"

"When I walked by it."

"Did you think it…peculiar that such a crater was to be seen there, in your favorite park?"

"Did you think it peculiar?" Jonathan asked.

"I did, I thought it was very interesting. You see, I specialize in this, in stars, the cosmos, outer space, whatever you want to call it. I work at the intersection of the universe and our humble little planet. It's my job to protect the latter. So, naturally, you are safe to assume I get nervous when I see a giant crater has formed in our park. Did you see what caused the crater?"

Jonathan shook his head.

"What was your reaction to seeing the crater? What was going through your mind?"

"I thought, 'Interesting!'"

"Anything else?"

"No, sir."

"Did you take a picture of it with your phone? Surely you did."

"No, I don't have a cell phone."

"You don't have a cell phone…"

Jonathan shook his head.

"Well, tell me what else you were doing that day."

"I went to the café…"

"Yes."

"And I went back through the park to get to my home."

"Now, Jonathan, looking at your identification here I see that you live on 45th Street. That's in The University District. I know just the place."

"Okay."

"So what were you doing across town at Capitol Hill?"

"The truth is I really like their coffee. It's the best in all of Seattle."

Agent Gray laughed. "An audacious claim. I like it. How do you get around? Do you drive a car?"

"No, I take the bus."

"I see."

"So let me see if I got this straight: you woke up, took the bus over to Capitol Hill, romped through Volunteer Park, saw the crater, went about your merry way to the café, and then went back through the park again. Didn't you feel frightened when you saw the crater? Did it really make sense to go back through the park again after you knew something had collided with the surface of the earth, leaving a deep impact?"

"Well, you see," Jonathan began, "I saw the crater, so I knew that whatever had struck the Earth was already gone and well on its way. So I knew it was safe to go through the park."

"Oh?"

"Yeah. The crater is the leftover mark of something. It isn't a hazard, more like a clue. You do like to deal in clues, don't you, Mr. Willows?"

"Why, yes, I do enjoy clues. Which leads me to my next question."

"Go for it."

Agent Gray Willows was smirking, not the way friends do, but more in a menacing way. "I, too, like the café by Volunteer Park. They have great croissants. That very morning, the morning you walked by the crater, I went there also. And you know what? That's not even the most interesting thing about this. You see, I noticed something else."

"What was that?"

"What I noticed, was that the barista who had been working was horrified. He said a fellow came into the café lifted up some sort of crystal shard, and used it as legal tender. Would you care to elaborate on this point? I cross-referenced the description of what this fellow looked like, and it sounds like he and you are one. Would you care to explain?"

"Well, I, um, I collect crystals."

"You do?"

"Yes, and I was short on money that day, so I tried to use it to pay for my coffee."

"The barista said the crystal shard you brought was roughly the size of a small child. How do you explain this?"

"I found the crystals in a cave when I was sperlunkling."

"Oh?"

"I found a bunch of crystals."

"Where? What cave?"

"The Cave of the Crystals."

"And where is that?"

"It's in Colorado."

Little did Jonathan know, there in fact was a Cave of the Crystals, located in Naica in Mexico.

"The Cave of the Crystals," Agent Gray continued, "is located in North-Central Mexico, not Colorado."

"Oh, I must be getting my caves mixed up. I sperlunk a lot."

"You mean, 'spelunk.'"

"Yes," Jonathan was feeling irritated now. "I think my explanation is quite clear. I brought with me my own form of money, bought some coffee, and continued with my day. Any more questions?"

"Crystals," the Agent said, his tone still calm and level, "are not an accepted form of currency anywhere. So, why did you try to use it?"

"I thought it had collector's value. I thought the barista might be interested in it."

"Well, removing the food and safety hazard of having crystal sprinkles on the donuts and crystal chunks in the coffee, the fact remains that what you did was very…suspicious."

"Did I commit a crime?"

"No, Jonathan Celestial, you did not. That much is true. A minor offense, yes. But a crime? Not quite."

There was a pause. The Agent was smiling. "The crystal sample is currently being analyzed at the laboratory. It may take a few weeks to analyze it. At this time, however, I have no more questions to ask of you."

Jonathan stood up and reached out to once more shake his hand. The Agent shifted his posture, standing up more straight. "Please know, Mr. Celestial, that I am a very, very diligent Agent. If there is something ever hidden, or covered, it is my aim to find it, to uncover it. I work tirelessly to keep our city, and our world, safe. Anyone or anything that stands in the way of our safety is an enemy to me. Please know that I will be following-up with you regarding this matter. I will be searching through every channel. I—"

"Yes, I understand," Jonathan said. "You don't have a work-life balance."

"You're funny!" The Agent cried. "Listen, Mr. Celestial, I know that this ID you brought in is fake. I can see through it. Whatever your real name is, please know I

WILL find it out. But for now, that's all the time I have to discuss these things with you. I would like you to know that I will be contacting you in a week or so for a follow-up interview as the nature of this crater becomes more clear."

"That's my ID."

"Well it's mine now. Sorry, Mr. Celestial. I'm afraid you will have to proceed nameless for now. Good day!"

Jonathan was led to the door. He stepped outside and walked across the busy street to the café where Blaine was reading.

"How did it—"

"He wants me to come back in a week," Jonathan answered.

"A week? Well, he didn't arrest you, so I suppose it could be worse."

"Yeah, I guess you're right."

They walked towards the bus stop.

That night, Jonathan opened the book and once more hoped to glean what it had to say about humanity:

The pursuit of justice, in some human societies, is noble, if problematic. Though most humans would attest that living in a just society is important to them, few would say that they do, in fact, live in just such a society. This disconnect demands further review. For now, it is noteworthy to observe that humans have a remarkable aptitude for treating one another in a cruel manner. Virtues of compassion and forgiveness rarely find their way into the justice systems, and the lofty goal of reforming a human being seldom are the destination. Rather humans seem bent on punishing one another through violent, horrendous acts.

"You okay?" Blaine asked.

"I'm okay. I just need to—"

"Decompress?"

Jonathan nodded.

"One more thing."

"What's that?" Blaine asked.

"The Agent knew my ID was fake. Better go with someone else next time."

"Shoot. Really?"

"Uh-huh."

"That's surprising to me. Well, listen Jonathan. I know that no matter what you didn't commit any crimes. You may be a bit eccentric, but I know you're a good person."

"You mean it?

"Mean what?"

"That I'm a person?"

"Of course! Boy, you're strange."

Jonathan hugged Blaine and patted him on the back. "Now get to bed, Mr. Celestial! In a couple days we head out on a camping trip."

"Okay!"

In bed, Jonathan thought about the Agent, how he had been so confident, so intimidating. What was this Agent hoping to discover? All Jonathan wanted was to find hope and healing. He didn't mean to hurt anyone. He wanted to be reconciled to his past. So he had created a massive crater in the middle of an urban park? Big deal, thought Jonathan.

Jonathan rose from the bed and looked out the window, towards the cosmos. His thoughts wandered, until they focused on that event that happened so long ago. All of a sudden, he felt his head become hot. His heart was beating quickly, as though it was going to leap out of his aching chest. It felt as though he couldn't handle the moment, and he began to fear he was going to fall over and pass out.

He groaned and held onto the window sill.

A few seconds passed, and then the panic was gone. He climbed back into bed, wondering if this in fact was what it really felt like to be alive.

DAY 10

It happened when Jonathan Celestial walked out of the shower.

With a towel draped around his skinny body, he quickly shuffled out of the bathroom. As he turned around, he heard Blaine's voice:

"Morning, Jonathan. Hey, you know, once you're dressed, I'd like to sit down and talk to you about something."

Jonathan put on a flannel shirt and dark jeans. Slowly, he went over to the table. Blaine was seated, his expression neutral.

"What is it?" Jonathan asked.

In Blaine's hands was Jonathan's book.

Jonathan said, "What are you—"

"What is this?" Blaine asked, opening the book and leafing through it. "You left it out last night."

"So?"

"Well," Blaine put the book down on the table. "I was reading through it. You see, there are sections that say things like 'To us stars' and 'for stars' along with 'in accordance with star law'." Then Blain turned to look up at Jonathan. "What the heck is this?"

"It's just a book—"

"I'm not an idiot, Mr. Celestial. The bizarre super powers, the weird name. Are you…are you…" Blaine sighed. "I can't even say it."

Jonathan cleared his throat. "Say what?"

Blaine leaned in towards Jonathan. "Are you some kind of being from space?"

Jonathan had no idea how to respond. For days he was dreading this inevitable moment. The question persisted in his head as to whether or not he would be accepted as he was. With sweaty palms and his heart beating in his head, he spoke:

"Okay, I guess I have some explaining to do."

Blaine put his hands on the table. "Yeah, I think so, too."

Jonathan rose from the table, walked over towards the window, and spoke:

"Like I already told you. My name is Jonathan Celestial. For a billion years, I worked in this galaxy as a star, lighting up the night sky. One day, something horrible, terrible, awful happened to me. I am still struggling to make sense of it. I can't even really talk about it, to be honest."

Blaine stared at Jonathan and did not look away. "I don't understand what you're saying. You mean to tell me that you're a star? But you're a person!"

Jonathan looked at his hand, at the lines on it. "I used my PTO to come to earth and—"

"PTO?"

"Paid Time—"

"I know what PTO is, Jonathan. I guess I just wasn't aware that the cosmic bodies had it."

"Well we do. I worked for a billion years, hating my life. All the other stars were so mean and cruel to me." He sighed. "I guess the best way to put it is to say that I never felt like I belonged as a star. So I used my vacation time to come here, as a human. But ever since I got here, I've been getting into trouble. This Agent guy is hunting me down. If he locks me away, I'll never find it."

"Find what?"

Jonathan looked out the window of the apartment. "What I am looking for is some meaning to my life, a source of restoration. You see, ever since I laid my eyes on this little blue and green planet called Earth, I have felt convinced that I would find what I was seeking here and here alone. That's why I came here as a human: to make peace with my past."

Blaine was staring at the table.

Jonathan walked over and sat again. "What?"

"I…"

"I know it's a lot."

"I don't know what to say. It's crazy. I've been secretly housing a star who is the subject of a governmental investigation. Wonderful!"

"I guess life is full of surprises."

"Got that right. So that leads me to my next question."

"Which is?"

Blaine smiled. "You know, I've really enjoyed getting to know you. Sure your acting methodology is not the best, but you're a good person, and I mean that, as weird as it sounds. So my question, I guess, is how can I be here to support you?"

Jonathan's face lit up. It was a bright, luminous display. "You mean, you're not going to kick me out?"

"Kick you out? Jonathan…we're friends."

Jonathan ran around the table and hugged him. Blaine was reluctant to hug, but finally decided to put his arms around Jonathan. "So you're a star? I've heard of stranger things. Okay, maybe I haven't. But that doesn't mean that this isn't anything we can't manage."

"I'm so glad to hear you say that. It makes the beating thing in my chest soar, so to speak."

"Your heart. Listen, I'm going to work with my friends to help you find what you're looking for. What you're looking for is kind of vague, but I want to be a part of helping to locate it."

"You're the best."

"No, you're the best."

"Well, okay then," Jonathan replied.

Blaine shrugged. "I'm just a barista in a post-rock band. But what I do have are friends, that and some determination."

"And that just might be enough."

"But you know what? You never told me much about your interview with the Agent, only that he wanted you to come back."

"Not much else to report."

"Well, listen, Jonathan. It's very important that you are…discrete in how you conduct yourself going forward."

"What do you mean?"

Blaine set the book on the table. "Well, if the public find out that there is a star secretly dwelling among them, not everyone may be as welcoming as I am. Humans tend to fear that which is different than them, that which is unknown. What with your space powers you are something of an unknown entity. You're well-meaning and harmless, but people are quick to draw conclusions." Blaine sighed, and then looked at Jonathan with a stern expression. "It is very important that you keep things secret, that you don't stand out at all."

"True enough. But I can't just sit here in your apartment all day. How will I ever find what I am looking for?"

Blaine chuckled. "I'm not advocating that. I'm just saying that it's important that you are…thoughtful about how you conduct yourself. We won't tell any of my friends, at least not now."

"Okay."

"How much PTO do you have?"

"I have…thirty days total."

"Really?"

"Yeah. Not bad, huh?"

Blaine stood up. "For a billion years of work? Yeah, that's pretty bad."

Jonathan continued to sit still at the table. He was attempting to process the fact that a human accepted him for who he was. He felt like a weight was lifted from his shoulders.

"So, what are we doing today?" he asked.

Blaine started laughing.

"What?" Jonathan continued. "I thought we were done with that line of conversation."

"I suppose so. Today I have a rehearsal with the band. You want to crash?"

"Oh, I already crashed when I landed on Earth."

"No, Jonathan. Do you want to come to the band rehearsal?"

"Sure!"

Blaine had a sip from a glass of water. "You really are a star. Wow."

•••

Mitch was playing the cymbals of his drum set gently, with brushes, allowing the sound to swell and swell. Tim, meanwhile, was laying down the chord progression which Blaine played against. Hypnotically, elegantly, with a subtle touch and restraint, Blaine was playing along on his guitar, occasionally trying out different pedals. The band felt less like a group of musicians than a fantastic dream unfolding before Jonathan. He sat in the corner of the room, watching them. All at once, Blaine stopped playing He turned to look at the paper in front of him. Shortly after, Tim and Mitch stopped playing as well. Blaine was writing something on the paper in front of him.

"When he stops playing," Rob said, pointing at Blaine, "The others usually catch on pretty quickly." Rob crossed his crossed his left leg over his right.

"It's all so wonderful," Jonathan said, beaming.

Blaine continued writing, then looked over at Jonathan. To Jonathan, he looked frustrated.

Then Blaine turned to face the other two musicians. "It's a bit sleepy-sounding, I think. Mitch, can you speed it up? Add some toms in there, too, please. Tim, feel free to play louder."

Once again Tim and Mitch were playing. Blaine didn't immediately start playing, but stood still, listening to what was being played. He closed his eyes, nodded a few times, and then jumped into the music with his guitar figure.

Rob, meanwhile, was making notes in his little book.

"Is this song on the new album?" Jonathan asked.

"No, it's totally new."

"What are you writing?" Jonathan pointed at the book.

"Oh," Rob scratched his forehead. "Making notes about the video."

"You mean the one about the farmer?"

"Gardener. And yes."

Jonathan's eyes lit up. "Let me see if I remember: the gardener spreads seeds, the boy gives a flower to a girl, and then what?"

"That's what I'm trying to figure out."

"You haven't figured it out?"

"The emotions in the music, in my thinking, go a lot of different ways," Rob put the pen up above his ear. "If the girl takes the flower, we could film them running through a field of flowers together. In fact, he could pick her up, hug her, you know, show love towards her."

"Sounds good to me!"

"Or," he grabbed the pen and used it as a bookmark. "We could have the girl take the flower, look at him in the eyes, and then cast away the flower, walking off. This would leave the boy alone in the field of flowers. The camera could slowly zoom out, revealing a larger and larger field, until he completely disappeared from view." Rob turned towards Jonathan. "What do you think?"

"What's the meaning of the second ending?"

Rob crossed his right leg over his left. "Meaning? Well, here's what I think: I think—"

"Oh wait. I think I get it. The gardener, which is kinda like God, creates all this beauty in the form of the flowers. A human tries to take this beauty and share it, only to find that he is unable to truly express what he is thinking and feeling to another human using God's creation. He is then left to be by himself, surrounded in beauty, but unable to understand or enjoy it."

Rob looked up from the note he was making in his book. The band was still playing. Blaine appeared quite focused, watching the other two bandmates scrupulously. The music echoed through the room.

"I like it," Rob answered. "Here's what I think: The gardener could be any of us. In sowing seeds, he is spreading acts of love and compassion. The boy, who also could be any of us, is captivated by this love and compassion, and brings it to the girl. She, however, needs to encounter love and compassion on her own, in her own time, in a way that makes sense to her. I guess what it means is that the two of them are not speaking the same language. The boy, meanwhile, is left to be in the field, to feel the love and compassion of God and to meditate on it until a girl comes along who he can truly connect with."

"Interesting," Jonathan replied, still watching the band play. "I think our perspectives are pretty similar. I like the second idea for the ending better, to be honest."

Rob was looking at the ceiling. "I am drawn to that one as well. We'll see what the band thinks. Or rather, we'll see what Blaine thinks. In case you couldn't tell, he's the dominant creative force in the band."

"That doesn't surprise me. It's neat that Blaine allowed me to come to his practice. I'm really seeing another side of him. He's so…serious when he's working on music."

"Yes," Rob assented, "but when the music is flowing and going well? He smiles in a way that you'll never see him smile anywhere else."

"Now that is something I'd like to see!"

Rob watched the band play. Blaine signaled for them to stop. "Me too," Rob said.

That night, Blaine and Jonathan talked for hours, Blaine sitting at the table and Jonathan on the futon that made squeaking noises every time he got on or off it. They were up late, laughing, occasionally quiet, and then, just as Comrade Sun was breaking through the horizon, Blaine, feeling bold asked, "So what is it you are looking for?"

"I already told you: purpose, meaning, and hope. Healing, really."

"Well, what are you hoping to be healed from?" Blaine looked squarely into Jonathan's eyes.

"Okay, if you want to know, I'll tell you a story…"

Day 11

Two young stars watched the clock eagerly. The bell rang, and they left the Star Academy together. Floating through space, through the Milky Way, which was their home, Albert Bright turned to Jonathan Celestial and spoke:

"Another snooze fest today, huh."

Jonathan shrugged. "I enjoyed the lecture on how humans eat and prepare food. I thought it was valuable."

They passed a neighbor and said hello.

Albert turned to Jonathan. "You just can't wait to be a working star. You can hardly contain your excitement to be in the same galaxy as Earth. If you could, I bet you'd take Comrade Sun's job in a beatheart."

"The human expression you are looking for is 'heart beat'. And yes, I would love to have the job of shining down on the Earth, being the source of its days and nights. Maybe one eon."

"You…you love humans, don't you?"

Jonathan cleared his throat and moved to the side to allow a string of other stars to pass by. "I think humans are the most peculiar things. Their lives are so short, so precious, and yet how many of them ever really think about such a thing?"

"Not many. They take their short lives for granted, and then poof! They're gone," Albert said.

"Same with us," Jonathan said. "A couple billion years go by like with the snap of a finger, and then we're white dwarves."

"What's the snap of a finger?"

"I'll explain later."

They reached a spot where they could see many lightyears of space before them. There were stars all throughout, working hard to luminously display their might. Not far off was Comrade Sun, who was a particularly well-respected and revered figure in many galaxies. There were other planets: Mercury and Venus to name two, but they weren't quite as compelling to Jonathan as Earth.

Jonathan's face was filled with awe. "Earth is just so teeming with life. It has oceans of life, skies with life, grassy fields with life. All of it is so wonderful to think about!"

"Then don't think about it," Albert smirked.

But Jonathan was stuck in his place, admiring the view.

"Come on, Jonathan," Albert said. "Let's get going."

"Okay, fine."

They were going to head to their posts when Jonathan stopped and said, "Albert, I have an idea."

"What is it?"

"How about we go wandering?"

"Wandering where?"

"Let's go somewhere new."

"Andromeda?"

"No, silly. I don't want to go to the same old stomping grounds. I want to go somewhere fresh."

"What are stomping grounds?"

"They are….oh, never mind."

With that, Jonathan began floating away from Albert, towards a dark direction. There were many less stars to be seen. Albert had to hurry to keep up:

"Space really is dark. It's hard to imagine what the shadows were like, before Sir Cosmos and the Star Keeper created stars."

"Well, I imagine it was dark. Dark and quiet. Quiet and dark." Jonathan replied.

"Indeed."

Jonathan turned around to look at Earth once more. "You know, Sir Cosmos says it's the only planet that hosts life. Can that really be true?"

"If Sir Cosmos said it, then it's true."

"We stars spend all day granting wishes and lighting up darkness," Jonathan continued. "Why has no star ever explored Earth?"

"How would that work?"

"I mean, what if a star fell to Earth and became imbued with life."

"'imbued with life'?"

"You know, a star living as a human," Jonathan finished.

"You could be the first one."

"Or you could be!"

"Hah, I would never go to Earth," Albert replied. "If I get assigned to the Milky Way, I'll probably just grant wishes to spoiled, privileged people. Keep my distance."

"I'd love to visit Earth," Jonathan said. "I'd love to see all the life that there is, to bask in it."

At that moment, the Star Keeper appeared.

"Why, hello you two. How are things?" he asked the two young stars.

"All is well," Jonathan replied.

The Star Keeper looked incredulous. "Any mischief?"

Albert sighed and said, "No, sir. We were just heading back to work on our studies."

"Very good. Did I hear you talking about Earth?"

Albert said, "No, we-"

"Yes, you did," Jonathan interrupted. "It seems like the most marvelous place."

Looking at Earth, and then back at the two stars, The Star Keeper replied, "I've been supervising stars who work in The Milky Way for eons. Earth's a pretty young planet. But I suppose it's all a matter of how you look at it. Anyway, it's a dreadful place."

"Dreadful?" Jonathan looked disappointed.

"I'll go into it more some other time. For now, you two best focus on your studies."

"Yes, Star Keeper," Albert and Jonathan said in unison as they floated past him.

On and on the two stars traveled. Soon, they were out of the Canis Major Dwarf Galaxy, and well on their way into darkness. Fewer stars could be seen on the horizon; Comrade Sun was no longer visible. Whereas Jonathan was feeling confident and adventurous, moving swiftly through space, Albert was dragging behind.

"Hey, Albert!"

"What?"

"Try and keep up." Jonathan was floating in a zig-zag pattern.

Then Jonathan came to a stop.

Albert caught up to him. "What is it, Jonathan?"

Jonathan looked up and said, "You see it? It's the Messier 87 galaxy. Isn't it a dark, lonesome place?"

The two stars floated there in space, all alone.

Suddenly, a bright spot on the horizon lit up. Red, green, blue, and purple, it was a dazzling display of luminous, swelling energy. Jonathan and Albert looked at each other.

"The gravitational core of a big star is collapsing," Jonathan whispered. "It's…"

"A supernova," Albert finished. "Jonathan, let's turn back."

"But if we go closer, the views will only get better."

"Jonathan, it's dangerous."

Jonathan turned towards Albert. "Are you afraid?"

Albert replied, "No, I'm not afraid. I just don't want to end up a white dwarf."

"There's no need for fear. The only star that's dying this eon is that one creating the beautiful views there in the distance. Come on; we won't get too close.

Jonathan floated towards the supernova. Reluctant, Albert slowly followed.

The colors of the supernova appeared more vivid as they approached what was one star's demise. Shock waves of star material, the remnants of the star, were being ejected at a speed one-tenth of light.

Still moving closer, Jonathan started zig-zagging to dodge shock waves. Albert, anxious, was just behind. The sound of the exploding star was deafening.

"Jonathan…"

"We're still pretty far from it, Albert. Don't be such a dimwit."

"Jonathan…"

A shock wave struck Jonathan and hurled him far off, millions of miles from Albert. All at once, the supernova was unfolding right before them. Jonathan began moving with all the might that his nuclear fusion would allow. But the waves were overtaking him. He felt one strike him and then another. In agonizing pain, he cried out:

"Albert! Where are—"

But the shock waves silenced him. Rosy, green, blue, and purples streaks of light sped past Jonathan. The sound was so loud he couldn't process what was happening to him.

Then, in one final push, Jonathan sped along, using the last of his energy. Still he was struck again and again by waves.

Turning around, he looked for Albert. There was no sign of him.

"Where are—"

A large powerful wave of energy struck Jonathan, and with that, he went dim for a time.

•••

"No mischief, huh, Mr. Celestial."

Jonathan looked up and saw Sir Cosmos himself. Jonathan turned to look one way and then the other.

"Where is?"

"It's a good thing I found you," Sir Cosmos continued, his eyes filled with compassion.

"Albert, I've got to go find Albert." Jonathan rose, as though to float back towards the supernova.

"A supernova, Mr. Celestial, is nothing to take lightly. True, it is a beautiful thing, but it is a deadly thing. It is the beauty of death itself."

"Where's Albert?" Jonathan screamed.

Sir Cosmos continued, apparently unfazed:

"You say you want to go to Earth. You work hard in your Human Studies course. Head of the class. Then what do you do? Head into an explosion." Sir Cosmos lowered himself to Jonathan's level and said, "The truth is I understand what drew you in. This universe is the most amazing thing. I'm glad you're okay. A constellation is currently searching for Albert, but in all honesty it looks grim."

"You mean—"

"I mean that Albert might…"

Jonathan begin shaking, his voice hoarse. "My fault. It's my fault."

Sir Cosmos put a hand on him. "Jonathan…" he said, his voice tender.

Jonathan screamed, "He told us to go back, but I insisted we go forward! He was right!"

Again Sir Cosmos said, his tone gentle and light, "Jonathan…"

Sir Cosmos held Jonathan Celestial in his arms. Reactively, Jonathan shook until he was out of Sir Cosmos' arms. Then he floated away, back towards the shadows.

"Wait, Jonathan! There is something I wish to share with you."

DAY 12

They drove along winding roads, farther and farther up a hill, below them an expanse of trees. The canopy of branches was bright green. Jonathan Celestial was gazing out the passenger window of the car, in awe, amazed at what he was seeing. The trees, it seemed, spread outward endlessly, as far as the horizon. Only other hills prevented him from seeing what lay far out.

"Incredible…inexplicable…inspiring."

"Having fun?" Blaine asked, not looking away from the road.

"It's all so much to take in," Jonathan replied. "I have looked upon Earth thousands of times, and seen how green it was. But I never have seen that greenery up so close like this."

"It's just trees, man," Tim said. "This guy kinda talks in a funny way."

"Is it 'just trees'?" Rob challenged.

Blaine had one hand on the steering wheel, and was sipping coffee with the other. "Now, you all know that the vision of Static Sea is to find the profound in all things. If anything, my friend Jonathan here is fully embodying the posture we should all have towards the natural world."

Tim replied, "I suppose you're right. But still, don't you think his reaction is a little, I don't know, over-dramatic?"

"I don't think that in the slightest," Blaine said, "and if you want your playing abilities to reach their full potential, I think it would be wise for you to approach things with a little more reverence, like my friend here."

Tim sighed. "Whatever you say, boss."

It had been Blaine's idea to take his closest friends on a camping trip. In preparation for their upcoming tour, it made sense to him to commune once more with the natural world. It was his hope that he could channel some of Jonathan's wonder and awe, which seemed to radiate from him so freely and unconditionally. Blaine also thought some time outdoors might aid Jonathan in his search. However, he was having a rough time. There was a lot going through his head, things that no doubt would come up while talking around the campfire.

When they reached the campgrounds, Jonathan hopped out of the car and began to climb the nearest tree.

Holding on to a branch as though for dear life, he was only a few feet off the ground. He could smell the bark, the leaves on the tree. He lingered there for a while, and then fell to the ground. When he got up, he noticed that a small crater was formed.

A few minutes passed and the tent was put together.

Jonathan jumped through the opening and collided with the entrance flap. He lay on the ground.

"Need some help?" Blaine unzipped and lifted the netting flap.

Inside the tent, Jonathan found a corner, where he placed his backpack, which Blaine had persuaded him to pack. He lifted out his book, along with his pajamas. He also took out a star fruit.

Blaine poked his head inside the tent and saw the fruit. "Where did you—"

"Don't worry," Jonathan said. "It's nutritious." He took a bite.

Outside of the tent the voices of Tim and Mitch could be heard. They were talking to someone"

"Everything is fine, sir."

"Thanks for checking on us. We don't know what created it."

Then a new face appeared inside the tent. It was the park ranger. "How are we doing, boys?" he asked.

Blaine said, "All is well. Is anything the matter?"

The park ranger pulled up his pants and said, "Well, I heard complaints of a loud explosion sound. I was looking around your campsite, and I noticed there appears to be a crater not far from that tree over there," he pointed. "Do you know anything about this?"

Jonathan Celestial's mouth was filled with star fruit. "Interesting…that is interesting! What on earth could have created it?"

Blaine turned to look at him, then back at the ranger. "I don't know what caused that crater-like thing out there, sir. But I'm sure whatever caused it won't be doing it again."

"Now how do you know that?" challenged the ranger. "There could be a wild animal on the loose."

"How would a wild animal create that?" Blaine asked.

"I don't know. Do you have a better explanation?"

"No, sir, I don't." Blaine was resolute in lying to protect his friend.

"Okay, well, know that if you need anything, I'm just over at the lodge." The ranger handed Blaine a folded up piece of paper. "Here's a map. I'm over here, on the eastern side."

"Thank you, sir," Jonathan said, juice from the star fruit dripping out of his mouth.

The ranger saluted. "Is that star fruit?"

"Pike Place Market."

"You boys from Seattle?"

"You bet we are!"

"Well, now. If you city slickers run into any trouble, just give me a call. I'd hate for whatever created *that* to return." He was pointing at the crater.

Blaine said, "We will keep you in mind. Thank you very much."

The ranger pulled on the brim of his hat and then left.

Furiously, Blaine grabbed Jonathan's shoulders and pulled him close. "Look, Jonathan. You absolutely have got to stop with the crater business. It's a dead giveaway that something is up. You know, you may have friends in the form of us, but if society and the world finds out that you exist, you could be in big trouble. Can you get that through your head?!"

"I was just getting down—"

"No, you weren't. You fell to the ground like a crashing meteorite. You want to be a human? Well, here's a good guiding principle for you. Guiding Principle #1: Human's don't make craters. Okay? Sound good?"

"Sounds good," Jonathan answered. "I have a question."

"What?"

"If that ranger, or the Agent guy, find out who I am, how quickly would other people find out?"

"All it would take is one picture or video. It could go viral," Blaine answered.

"What does that mean?"

"What it means," Blaine continued, "is that news of your star-ness would spread like a virus. Who knows how people would react? If history has taught humans any-thing, it's that being different leads to getting into trouble." He smiled. "So don't be different."

Jonathan ran a hand through his hair. "You...you didn't tell anyone else about me, or my story, did you?"

Blaine sighed. "No, I did not. Your identity is safe with me."

Later that night, after dinner, the friends were assem-bled around a fire.

"So how is it going? It's been about two weeks?" Tim asked Jonathan.

Blaine nodded.

"Two weeks since what?" Jonathan blurted out.

"Since you two guys met," Rob said, looking up.

Jonathan looked at Blaine. "It was about two weeks ago that I first saw you guys perform. You really impressed me!"

Mitch laughed.

Blaine said, "No need to get overly praiseful. We're just a band, playing songs for anyone who will listen."

"And where did you say you were from?" Tim asked.

Jonathan paused. "I'm from Spokane."

Blaine nodded more.

"What has been the most striking thing about your time here?" Tim asked.

"Oh, nobody has struck me."

Mitch laughed. "What are you learning from being a Seattleite?"

"I don't know. That's a complicated question."

"That's okay. I just thought I would ask. It's always good to connect."

"Connect? What do you mean?"

"That's what humans do, Jonathan," Blaine said, aware that nobody else knew the truth. "They get together, eat, laugh, cry, and most of all, just talk about what is going on. They try to make sense of things."

"I see what you mean." Jonathan pointed up at the sky. "Look! Some constellations."

"Which ones do you see?" Blaine asked.

"Well, there's the Big Dipper," he pointed. "But that's an easy one. There's Circinus…Libra..and Lupus."

"Whoa," Tim said. "You found those quickly. Where is —"

"And when in doubt, whenever I feel lost, or lonely or confused," Jonathan continued, "I look to the great navigator: the North Star."

"Now, that's one I have heard of," Blaine replied.

Jonathan walked over to where the map was folded up, on the picnic table. "Is there anywhere around here where I can see the stars a little bit better?"

Blaine walked over and held the map for him. "Listen, you might want to downplay the star stuff. I made up the Spokane story for you. You're a struggling actor from the Inland Empire, remember?"

"Blaine?"

"Yes, Jonathan?"

"This is going to sound bizarre. I never thought I'd say this, but I actually miss the land of the stars a bit."

"I thought you said they all hated you after what happened. You said they were cruel to you."

Jonathan sighed. "Most of the stars in the night sky don't think highly of me. But there are exceptions. There's the Star Keeper, The North Star, Comrade Sun, The Moon, The Big Dipper, and Sir Cosmos of course. Together, this group of celestial beings are my main allies. But yes, there are not many stars I can really talk to. I guess I just miss space a bit. Do you think I could commune with The North Star for a bit?"

Blaine laughed. "Don't let me get in the way of your communion."

"Okay. It's just, this investigation has got me thinking I'll never find the restoration I am seeking."

Blaine looked right into Jonathan's eyes, illuminated by the campfire not far off. "Don't rule it out."

"So where is a good vantage point to see the North Star?"

Blaine pointed. "There's a hill right over—"

But Jonathan was already walking away from them, in the direction Blaine was pointing.

"I'll see you guys in a bit!" Blaine called, running to catch up to Jonathan.

"Shouldn't we wait?" Blaine asked.

"Why? Right now is the perfect time to meet with him."

"But it's dark."

Jonathan pointed with his finger, and light flickered out of it, much like a flashlight.

"And we'll get hungry…"

Jonathan reached into his pocket. "Star fruit?"

Through rows of trees, up a slope, the two friends moved. With authority, confidently, Jonathan marched. He passed under a tree branch and tripped. He fell onto the ground and rolled down the slope.

Blaine called out, "Are you okay?"

But Jonathan was laughing. "No crater this time."

At once Jonathan rose to his feet. He walked in between two trees and went up the slope to the top of a hill. Blaine followed closely behind.

Standing on top of the hill, the ground was flat. Up above their heads was the night sky, a tapestry of stars, the cosmos on full display. Jonathan looked up and sighed, smiling.

"It's beautiful," he said. "You know, I don't hold their cruelty against them. I just wish they treated me differently. I wish it felt—"

"Like home," Blaine finished.

"Right. Like home."

"Funny," Blaine remarked. "All this time you've been a stranger among beings different than you. For once, I feel like I'm the one who is among beings different than me."

Jonathan sighed. "You know, I feel like a stranger no matter where I go."

"That's a heavy load, Jonathan. Well, are you ready to—"

A beam of light shone down from the night sky. Jonathan slowly rose into the air, about twenty feet off the ground. The stars above began flashing.

"I'm being connected to his galaxy!" Jonathan cried.

"What?!"

Greetings, Jonathan. I have done the calculations; the methodology was sound. You will surely find that which you seek. Indeed, it is not far off.

Wonderful! How are you, North Star?

All variables considered, my status is favorable. Reciprocally, what is yours?

I feel better now that I am talking to you.

That is pleasing to hear. Jonathan, it is with theoretical certainty that I assure you that you will locate the variable you are pursuing. Though the definition of said variable eludes my understanding, my conclusion is that you will find it.

Great! What have you been doing?

The conditions of my regiment remain consistent. I navigate and assist those who remain disoriented on Earth. Such knowledge you already have.

True. It's just nice to hear from you. That's all.

Indeed. However, my idle time is nearly depleted, and so I must terminate this social interaction. Jonathan, may you fare well. I will direct you back to the coordinates of your peers.

Yes, please do.

Back on the ground, Jonathan turned to face Blaine, who was dumbstruck by what he saw and heard.

"What the—"

"That was the North Star," Jonathan said in excitement.

"Well, he was a bit hard to understand, but if you're happy, I'm happy."

Jonathan grabbed Blaine's arm and they ran down the hill. "He's going to guide us back."

"This is pretty crazy stuff," Blaine said, "but, man, is it cool. Where do we go from here?"

"I don' know. Hey, North Star?"

Salutations once more, Jonathan.

"Where do we go?"

Turn left at the big boulder.

They followed the directions of the North Star, one step at a time:

Turn right at the tree with the owl on the branch.

In 500 feet, turn left.

You are on the fastest route possible.

Turn right.

Finally, having reached the camp, Jonathan dove into the tent. He put on his pajamas, rolled over onto his side, and was asleep within minutes. Blaine looked at him, and then poked his head out of the flap of the tent. Looking up at the stars of the night sky, Blaine smiled.

Day 13

It was midday when they got back to Seattle from the camping trip. Blaine had to work the closing shift at Java City, and so Jonathan Celestial was free to spend his time as he pleased.

"Don't do anything too silly while I'm out," Blaine said to Jonathan as he left.

Taking a step out into the warm air, Jonathan looked in one direction and saw the university. Today, he thought, would be a good day to do something different, something novel. He crossed the street, towards where buses were passing by, and got on the first one he saw. He still had a small amount of money left. Walking through bus route number 47, looking for a seat, his mind was raging with anxious thoughts.

What Jonathan revealed to Blaine about the supernova all those millions of years ago was possibly the smartest, or most foolish, thing he had done yet in his time on Earth. There would be no way to undo the vulnerability that Jonathan expressed to Blaine, but at least in the act of telling the story he was able to process and reflect on the event from a new angle, a new perspective. Jonathan could see Blaine's expression, concerned and yet incredulous, as he told him what happened:

"I really don't know what to say, Jonathan," Blaine said. "I would say 'I'm sorry', but that doesn't do any justice to the severity of your experience."

A pause followed. Jonathan stared at him, desperate for Blaine to react, to show that he did, indeed, know what Jonathan was feeling.

All of a sudden, matter-of-factly, Blaine said, "So, effectively, what you are looking for on Earth is some healing from the guilt you feel. You feel like the ghost of…Albert?"

Jonathan nodded slowly.

"You feel like the ghost of Albert is hanging over you, following you everywhere you go, affecting what you do. Is that a fair assessment?"

"Yes. What I carry with me is hurt itself." Jonathan put a hand on his chest. "I carry this with me. None of the stars will talk to me, except for a few celestial beings. When the typical star does talk to me, it is with coldness and condemnation." Jonathan shook. "They *despise* me."

"Okay. Well, I'm all for traveling and finding yourself, but I just don't know how you will find a way to make peace with the past here on Earth. I'm not saying it's beyond finding. It's just…" Blaine leaned back in his chair at the table. "It's just that this world, Earth, is already completely full of enough hurt, and healing is hard to come by."

Jonathan looked determined. "I know I can find what I need here. I just need to be diligent. I need to change my approach. I need…"

"What you need, I think, is the support of others." Blaine leaned on his right hand. "I will be here to support you, until your PTO is up. I am prepared to do what I can, which is not much. Now, you might be wondering why I am so happy to help you. The truth is that there is a reason why, which I will tell you more about when the time is right. For now, let's just say that helping you helps me."

Jonathan smiled. "Thank you. I know with a little help I can process all of this. I look forward to hearing more about your story soon."

"Good."

"But at the same time," Jonathan said quickly, "I feel assailed by doubts. I have been reliving memories of the supernova since it happened, and that was a billion years ago."

"All you can do is try, right?"

"I guess so. But, Blaine…"

"What?"

Jonathan spoke in a soft tone. "I'm scared."

"What are you scared of?"

"I can't put words to it, but that's how I feel. It's like being sucked into a black hole until you're completely erased."

"I understand. I have a question."

"What is it?"

"At the end of the story, you said that Sir Cosmos wanted to tell you something before you left. Did you ever hear what had to say?"

There was a pause.

"I mean," Blaine laughed slightly, "there was a billion years between that point in time and now. Surely it came up."

"It did."

"So?"

Jonathan was not making eye contact. "He told me this: with every supernova, all the material necessary for a new star to form is laid bare in space, and all that needs to pass is some time before it happens."

"Okay. What do you make of that?"

Jonathan stood up from the chair, walked a few steps towards the window, and then looked right into Blaine's eyes:

"It pisses me off."

•••

"Hey, Weirdo!"

Jonathan looked up, no longer thinking back to that conversation, and saw Lyla sitting in the back seat of the bus with a book on her lap.

"Hi, Lyla."

"Of all the buses in this city…what are you doing?"

Jonathan approached her. "Can I sit next to you?"

"Absolutely not."

He turned around and heard her, his facial expression one of apprehension:

"I was kidding! Come; have a seat."

Seating himself slowly, Jonathan looked to see that she was reading a thick book.

"What are you reading?"

"*On Humanity.*"

"Good one."

Her eyes brightened. "I am! It's riveting!"

Jonathan folded his arms. "Where is this bus going, anyway?"

"You mean you got on a bus without knowing where it's headed?"

He nodded.

She began fidgeting with the flap of her book. "Wow. I would say you are a weirdo, but that's pretty well established at this point."

Feeling ambitious, Jonathan replied, "Tell me, why do you act this way towards me?"

"What way?"

"Oh, come one. You are sarcastic, and…" Jonathan remembered a word from his book. "You are sarcastic, and snarky. That's the word!"

She stopped fidgeting. "Well, in a general sense I find you to be a peculiar individual, and I feel that that peculiarity deserves to be treated appropriately."

"I see."

She smiled. "Why do you ask?"

"Oh, no reason."

She smirked. "You know you can ask me to discuss your peculiar nature any time. I am happy to do so. It brings me great joy."

Jonathan turned to look out the window of the moving bus. "Okay."

"Jonathan…it brings me great joy."

Now Jonathan was wishing he boarded a different a bus.

He felt a finger poke his shoulder. He looked at her. "This bus goes to West Seattle," She said.

"Got it. Thanks."

"What business do you have over there?"

Jonathan replied, "I'm looking for something."

"You mentioned that at the library. Something about hope? Good luck, pal." She leaned in close towards Jonathan. "The thing about looking for hope is that it's not always necessarily in our control whether we can find it or not, and often when we do come across it…" she clapped her hands. "It's gone!"

"That's encouraging. What I want to find is something that will bring me a sense of relief."

"Now that's slightly more specific. What are you really looking for? Tell me."

Already Jonathan felt embarrassed about revealing his starhood to one human, and he didn't intend to do so again, not Lyla.

"What I want…is to be able to look up at the stars at night and feel peace."

"Aww, poor Jonathan. You don't feel peace on a cosmic level?"

"No. That's a good choice of words."

"Of course it is; I said it." She brushed her hair behind her ears. "Well, here we are, on a bus, headed to West Seattle.

Buzzing through Jonathan's mind was an excerpt from his book concerning sarcasm:

Humans, particularly those of a higher intelligence or sensitivity, will utilize the art of sarcasm to convey truth in a veiled form. By speaking in one perverse, insincere way, these individuals express profound thoughts and feelings. While they may seem harsh, they in actuality are often very thoughtful and kind individuals who are simply struggling to make sense of reality.

The bus came to a stop. Lyla turned towards Jonathan:

"Here we are, Weirdo."

"Where?"

"Where? We're at the beach!"

Jonathan got up and followed her off the bus. It seemed as though everyone on the bus was getting off at this stop, for Jonathan had to wait a long time before he was able to leave. Once off, he noticed that Lyla was waiting for him.

"Care to stroll?" she asked.

"Don't you have somewhere you need to be?"

She smiled. "I am where I need to be. Take a walk with me."

Feeling he didn't have the option to decline, he said, "Okay."

Along a sunlit trail they walked. Her gait was slow, and so Jonathan was conscious of his own pace. Beneath their feet there was the shore, water lapping against the sandy edge.

"So you went camping, huh?" she asked.

Jonathan nodded.

"How was that?"

Jonathan turned to look at her. "Why do you care?"

"Just making conversation..." she mumbled.

"It was nice."

"Did you run into any bears?"

"What?"

She kicked a rock. "I asked if you saw any bears."

"No, I did not."

"Oh, well that's good. That could be trouble."

Jonathan looked at her, scrutinizing her.

She continued:

"I spent yesterday studying for a midterm. We are learning about constellations."

"Yeah? Which ones?"

She kicked the same rock as before. "Ones high up in the sky, in space."

"Got it."

"But in all seriousness, I do love learning about this stuff."

"That's good. Living with passion is important."

"I hear you are an actor?"

Jonathan puffed out his chest. "I am. I was in a commercial for a cleaning spray, and I'm going to be in the Static Sea music video, whenever they film it."

Her eyes got big. "Cool! You know I'm a fan of Static Sea. Nobody does post-rock like them."

"It's true."

The trail began to curve. There was a lull in the conversation.

Jonathan, growing ever more accustomed to social cues, asked, "What are you doing tomorrow?"

"Well, aren't you nosey!"

"I prefer 'inquisitive'."

Lyla looked at Jonathan. "I am going to a counter-demonstration tomorrow."

Jonathan felt an aching sensation in his chest.

"What is the demonstration about?" he asked, feeling dread.

Lyla answered, "You really are out of touch, aren't you? There was a big announcement about it in the papers and online. A couple weeks ago, out of nowhere, this big crater formed in the park. Nobody has any idea how it formed. Some think it was a meteorite. Others are a little more paranoid and think some alien has come to Earth and wants to destroy us all."

The aching in Jonathan's chest grew.

"Anyway," she continued, "Some people are going to make a scene and tell this 'alien' to go back home. People get afraid. People are stupid." She smiled.

Jonathan could hear the gentle sound of the water against the shore.

"That's the main demonstration," she said. "I am going to counter-demonstrate, telling them that there is no scientific reason to believe that an extra-terrestrial being is here on Earth. Also, that they are stupid. Also, even if there was an alien, who is to say that he would be a threat?"

Jonathan replied, "Indeed. Who is to say?"

"So I will be at Volunteer Park tomorrow around noon for that. Then, more studying." Suddenly, she stopped walking. "You know, I'd really like for an alien to come here to Earth. Everything gets so…boring. It'd be nice for something exciting to come and shake things up."

Jonathan took in a deep breath and exhaled. "I suppose that could be good," he answered.

"You want to go?"

"I don't know…"

"Well, I know you're a busy fellow, what with starring in cleaning spray commercials and spontaneously boarding buses, but it might be good for you to be a part of something bigger than yourself."

Jonathan was looking at the back of his hand. "Why would people assume that an alien has come, and that he is a threat?"

"What, do you think there's an alien?"

"I, er, I didn't say that. But if there was an alien…why would he want to hurt anyone? Maybe he's just exploring."

"This world is stupid and boring, full of stupid and boring people. That's why I was always drawn to space," she answered. "People fear what they don't know or understand. Knowledge is power. It's my job to educate people." She raised a fist in the air as she said this.

"Have fun with your education. I will see if I'm available."

Again she stopped walking. "You know, I know two things for sure: you are a huge weirdo, and I'm really glad I ran into you, that we went on this walk together."

"You are?"

She nodded. "I guess I kinda like spending time around you. Why? The answer to that question is as mysterious as a star in the sky."

"Thanks," Jonathan replied. "I guess."

DAY 14

"Wake up, sleepyhead."

Jonathan Celestial looked up into Blaine's face. He rose from his bed at once. Beams of radiant sunlight cascaded through his window, practically blinding him as his eyes adjusted.

"What…time is it?"

"12:00. But don't worry; it's the solstice."

"The solstice!"

"That's right. The longest day of the year. I'm sure you already knew that, though."

"For us stars, the solstice is an important day indeed! Both December 21st and June 21st."

"Yeah? How so?"

"Well, in December we stars put the emphasis of our work on the Southern Hemisphere of Earth. In June? It's the Northern Hemisphere."

"Well put."

Jonathan took off his pajamas and put on a shirt and shorts in a matter of seconds.

"Do you do everything rapidly?"

"Of course! So what are we doing today?"

Blaine looked around the room and then said, "Boy, you really are clueless. Today is the Solstice Parade, one of the biggest events in Seattle all year. There is a parade of dancers, bike riders, people in costumes, and tons of art and music. Static Sea will be playing at Gasworks Park."

"Sounds wonderful!"

"I'll have more of a sense for how the show's going to go down when I talk to the rest of the band later today, but for now, first thing's first: coffee."

"Coffee!" Jonathan screamed. He ran out of his room and bumped into the wall in the hallway. After rubbing his head, he went through the pantry.

"There's no coffee! There's no coffee!"

"We're going out for coffee. Come on."

Outside they stepped, into the warm air. Already the day was wearing on. People were out and about, walking and talking in groups, filling the streets. The two friends went towards 45th street and turned. They entered Java City.

They had a seat at a table with their drinks.

"All right, Jonathan, I want you to try and pace—"

Jonathan's cup was empty.

"Oh, geez…"

"I feel great! I feel awesome!"

Blaine turned his head to look out the large windows of the café. He saw the newspaper dispenser and was horrified by what he saw.

"One moment," he said to Jonathan.

On the cover of the newspaper, in clear color, was a picture of the crater.

Jonathan exclaimed, "That's—"

But Blaine put a hand over his mouth. "You're not making this easy on me, are you? Here: I will read the article out loud, but you aren't allowed to say a single word. Deal?"

"Um, okay. Deal."

"Okay." Blaine cleared his throat:

Who Created the Crater?
A Seattle Messenger Special Report

Some people say it was an incidental, environmental occurrence.

To others, an extra-terrestrial is here in Seattle, among us.

"I just saw the crater, and I was so scared," said Theodore Mason, an observer of the crater.

Agent Gray Willows, of the Bureau of Astral Anomalies, is heading the investigation into this environmental phenomenon. He is the leading source of information concerning the nature of the crater:

"At this time, we are undergoing a thorough, sweeping investigation," Willows told The Messenger. "We do not have a conclusion for the public at this time, but we advise people to take standard safety precautions, and to report all suspicious observations directly to the Bureau."

The Messenger will continue to offer coverage around the crater. Any public observations can be shared at the following number...

Blaine lowered the newspaper. Jonathan's looked curious. "That wasn't so bad," he said. "It could be worse."

"Come on, let's go," Blaine answered.

They walked through the street, heading down the slope.

Blaine said, "Despite our best efforts, the media is all over you. It's only a matter of time before this Bureau catches on to us. Oh man...this is bad, Jonathan."

"What we need to do," Blaine continued, "is come up with a plan. No doubt people are plotting right this very moment how to find and catch you. We need to be thinking two steps ahead."

"Like this?" Jonathan ran a few steps in front of Blaine, who replied, "Now is not the time for jokes. Listen, I have an idea. I'm thinking that maybe we can—"

But it was at that moment that the two friends realized they had walked onto the street where the parade was happening, cutting Blaine short.

There were people in costumes, with faces painted bright colors. Others were riding bikes. In the distance there was a marching band. Some people were roller-blading and wearing flowers. Then there were the costumes. There were people dressed as dragons, flowers, dogs, mermaids, birds, characters from movies, and lions to name just a few of the many costumes to be seen. In the air were colorful streamers. The sounds of people cheering and applauding, too, were loud.

Jonathan turned to face Blaine and asked, "What planet are we on now?"

"Great question."

They moved through the parade, filled with wonder by all that they saw.

Then Jonathan heard a chanting sound from behind.

"What's that?" He asked Blaine.

"I don't know, but it's getting louder."

A small group of people was walking towards the parade. One of the people was carrying a sign which read: NO ALIENS.

"It says—"

"I know what it says, Jonathan."

Jonathan Celestial walked innocently up to the group. "Hello. How's it going?"

"Get out of the way, man."

"Yeah!" the group called.

Blaine said, "We should really be going—"

"What are you doing today?" Jonathan asked the fellow holding the sign.

"We are protesting this event," he said confidently. "You see, it's events like this, The Fremont Solstice Festival, that are the reason our planet is now in danger."

"Danger?"

"Yes" a woman with a hoarse voice shouted. "The Space Menace has come to Earth and wants to annihilate all of humanity. We need to let him know that he is not welcome here."

"That's strange," Jonathan replied, "I wasn't under the understanding that the space guy wanted to annihilate anything."

"Well," the woman answered, waving the sign in her hand. "We heard it from the Bureau itself: a star guy has come to earth and wants to enslave all of us and take over! We must stop him!"

"Yeah!" the rest of the crowd called. "Stop him!"

Blaine interjected, "You just said he was going to destroy us. Now, you're saying he wants to enslave us? What does he exactly want to do? And didn't you read the report? He said there was no definitive conclusion at this time."

"You sound an awful lot like you WANT to be killed by the alien."

"What's your name?" Blaine asked.

"Henrietta. I'm the leader of the Anti-Space-Menace-Alliance-For-Making-Earth-Safe. We're nothing more than a group of people who are paying attention."

"But what did this space guy do to any of us, anyway?" Jonathan asked.

"It's clear what he's done: he's invaded our planet, and is on the loose. Say, the way you're talking about him is mighty suspicious."

It was at that moment that they heard another source of chanting. Another group of demonstrators were approaching.

Blaine put a hand to his face. "Oh, man. Who are you guys?

"Welcome the Alien! Welcome the Alien!"

At the front of the group was Dave, the eccentric fellow who had previously talked to Jonathan at the Static

Sea concert. "Name's Dave." He gestured skyward with is hands. "Mighty Extra-terrestrial, we don't know where you are, or what you have planned, but we want you to know that we welcome your life-giving energy into our world. Welcome!"

"Who are you?" Blaine asked.

"Why, we're the Task-Force-For-Meeting-And-Greeting-The-Cosmic-Presence."

"I like this group more," Jonathan said to Blaine.

"Do you have any idea what you're dealing with, here?" Henrietta asked Dave.

"I don't, but I do trust that it will be a good thing. We trust all things."

"This menace is an absolute threat to the stability of our society!"

"Well, maybe it's time for a new society, right boys?"

"Right!"

It was at that moment that the two groups began marching in circles, waving their signs, as Henrietta and Dave talked.

"Really," Dave said, "Alien, or Cosmic Presence, as we like to refer to it, is already inside of us all; all we need to do is to be attentive to it. He doesn't mean us any harm. I'm sure he's just looking to pass by in on an interstellar mission. Pretty righteous, if I may say so myself."

"The Alien is a menace, and must be either studied or eradicated before it eradicates us. This is a sign of the times. For too long, we humans have been asking for something from outer space to come to our planet. And here it is, somewhere in our own city." Henrietta turned to call out to the crowd. "If anyone knows any information about the being who created that crater, there will be a large monetary reward. Did I mention that it is large?"

Dave turned to Jonathan and patted him on the shoulder. "Brother, it's been too long. How is the journey? Really great to see that you've come out to support us. Means a lot to me."

"Oh, I didn't—"

"Didn't what?" Henrietta asked sharply.

"I didn't mean to support or oppose the Alien Extraterrestrial menace . I just wanted to get some coffee and enjoy a parade."

And so the groups continued to demonstrate, walking in circles, waving their signs. Others came to join both groups, which meant they expanded in size to the point of blocking the parade route.

A man in a baseball cap approached the two competing groups.

"Who are you?" Henrietta asked.

"Who are you?" Blaine asked.

"Hey, man," Dave said.

"Hi guys," the man in the baseball cap said. "I'm Floyd. I'm the chairman of the commission for the Fremont Solstice Parade. Now, I hate to rain on your parade, but well, you guys are all kinda raining on ours."

"What do you mean?" Henrietta snapped.

"The name-calling, the shouting, the demonstrating. This is not a political event. It's an opportunity to celebrate a natural phenomenon. "I'm going to have to ask you all to stop what you are doing immediately. Thanks, guys."

"But this isn't a political matter," Henrietta explained, "It's a moral one."

"Nay," Dave corrected, "it's a spiritual one."

"Well," Floyd continued, "whatever it is, it needs to stop. Children are here. Go on back to Westlake Center if you want to have an event."

Henrietta turned to her group and sighed. "All right. But you haven't heard the last from us. We'll be around!"

"Us too!" Dave called as his group disappeared.

Blaine turned to Jonathan. "Let's get out of here."

Jonathan said, "It seems like there are a lot of different reactions to me be being here. How interesting!"

"No, not interesting. Bad."

"Why bad?"

"Because, as the public outcry grows, and as the Agent looks for you, you're only more at risk." Blaine looked around and then continued:

"I need to head back down to the park. Static Sea's got a show to play!"

Jonathan nodded. Walking up to him, holding a sign, was Lyla.

She pointed at her sign and smiled. It read: BE REA-SONABLE

"How's it going, weirdo?"

Not in the mood for snarkiness, Jonathan replied, "Been better. I gotta go."

Back at *Eclipse*, he opened his book:

Humans possess the intriguing propensity for gathering in groups. When such a thing happens, often a singular ideology replaces any rational or critical thought, leaving the group to develop its own consciousness. It is often under such circumstances that a group positions itself in terms of its opposition to an enemy or other group. This use of the term "other" is worthy of note. Humans, it seems, have the ability to rigidly define themselves and to view others as being threats. In turn, these "threats" are caricaturized until they lose their humanity, thereby making it easier to oppose them.

Day 15

Waking up late, Jonathan Celestial ran into the kitchen of the apartment and prepared coffee. He sat at the table, taking in the strong aroma of his drink, thinking about the next day. They were going to film the music video for Static Sea's lead single, and it was decided that he was to play the boy who reaps the flowers. Reflecting on the larger meaning of this video, which still eluded him, he walked over to the window and gazed out at the city, scratching his head.

When he was ready to go out for the day, he locked up the door to the *Eclipse* apartment and went out. Blaine was working today, so he was given the freedom to do as he pleased.

Looking at the cracks in the sidewalk beneath his feet, Jonathan started thinking, wondering how things might have been different had he not insisted that Albert and he go towards that supernova all those years ago. Of course, they would still be friends. The other stars likely would still have liked him, instead of holding things against him. Though he was always interested in Earth and in humans, it is possible that if Albert hadn't been lost to the supernova Jonathan would never have come to Earth. Where would that have left him? Full of regret, ruing his decision to go into the supernova as moronic and most of all dangerous, Jonathan could feel his heartbeat picking up. He pressed the crosswalk button and saw that there was a slight tremor in his hand, that it was shaking. The feelings were returning, a sense that something was about to destroy him. He ran across the street intersection and kept going until the he felt himself calm down. He tried to get a sense of where he was in the city.

Nearby was a building with stained glass and bells. Inside, faintly, Jonathan heard the sound of voices singing. Curious, sensing that this connected to what he recalled studying about human religion, he entered the building.

A group of people were gathered, singing a lovely, harmonious hymn. Jonathan stood still, as though the moment demanded he stop whatever he was doing and simply bask in what was unfolding before him. In particular, he paid attention to the words they were singing:

O Lord, my God, when I in awesome wonder
Consider all the worlds Thy Hands have made
I see the stars, I hear the rolling thunder
Thy power throughout the universe displayed
Then sings my soul, my Savior God, to Thee
How great Thou art, how greatThou art

Deeply moved, Jonathan let his hands hang at his side. He breathed in deeply and exhaled slowly. Smiling, he continued to listen to them sing.

"It's about stars," he whispered.

Then, all of a sudden, the conductor stopped and so did the singers.

"All right, go ahead and take ten, everyone," the conductor said.

Jonathan walked up to the conductor, who was a short man with blonde hair and a bright smile.

"Hello," Jonathan said, "how are you?"

The conductor's smile grew bigger. He reached out a hand to shake with a gentle grip. "I am well. Welcome to our rehearsal."

"The music sounds great."

The conductor chuckled. "Thank you very much. After all, we are singing about how great someone is, so if our music can even remotely approach that, then I think we have done something worthwhile."

"It's wonderful! It's spectacular!"

The conductor folded his hands. "Thank you very much," he said.

"Is it okay if I sit here for the rest of the rehearsal?"

"Certainly. All are welcome here. Feel free."

Jonathan sat in one of the pews. He pulled out the book from the back of the pew in front of him, realizing that it was a Bible.

Once more, as he did every once in a while, he wondered: who created Sir Cosmos?

In the words of the hymn he heard a praise of this God, an awe directed towards Him. Jonathan didn't know how he felt about all of this. He looked around the sanctuary of the church, mesmerized by the stained-glass windows. He looked up and saw that the choir was singing again.

All his life, for more than a billion years, he had proceeded with the understanding that all celestial life began with Sir Cosmos. It always ended there. The curiosity of the larger meaning of it all captivated him, but he didn't know what the answers to his questions were. Here was a community of people who were directing reverence towards a being who was above all. But he was left to wonder who created God.

What Jonathan knew for sure was that these people in front of him embodied a sort of awe and wonder towards their deity, that they were living fully and wholly in the light that it brought to their lives. Jonathan desperately wanted to feel something like that.

To his thinking, Jonathan was living two sorts of lives. On the one hand, he was still living in fear and anxiety, too nervous to embrace life. On the other, he was succeeding in feeling the joyful ecstasy of being alive and having a preciously short existence. It felt like a contradiction to him, but thinking such a thing didn't change any-thing. This was his reality.

What he did know was that he wanted to live with more wonder in his life both as a human and a star. The mere thought of living as a star again caused him to sigh, to feel his fist clench tightly.

Jonathan shook his head and opened up the Bible. He leafed through it, ending up in a section called "Proverbs". He read the first bit of text that his eyes landed on:

> *Love prospers when a fault is forgiven, but dwelling on it separates close friends.*

He closed the Bible quickly and threw it on the ground. He stood up and walked out of the church.

A star celebration was held for Albert Bright shortly after Jonathan returned from the encounter with the su-pernova. Jonathan broke down when he spoke at this event, sobbing and shaking uncontrollably. He had to take a place in the audience without finishing the words he prepared. Surely, he loved Albert. They grew up together at the Star Academy, spending time together as they grew and learned. What Jonathan always longed for, desperate-ly, achingly, was to be able to be face-to-face with Albert, to be in his calming presence again. Then, in that mo-ment, he would beg him for forgiveness. Always he want-ed to ask for forgiveness for being so foolish and reckless, but never had he known what words he would have used to ask for it. Walking through the streets of Seattle on a sunny afternoon, Jonathan imagined facing Albert, know-ing that it would never happen. Albert was a white dwarf, and had been one for a billion years, somewhere in the far reaches of space. They would never see each other again, and this was a fact that Jonathan was still unable to ac-cept.

Clenching his fists, walking quickly, Jonathan thought about the bit he read in the Bible. Having read it felt like being slapped across the face.

"Does his inability to forgive me mean that I love him any less?" Jonathan whispered.

The "fault" in the verse was Jonathan's foolishness. He wondered: Was he dwelling on it? Was every action he took in his life since that supernova simply a reaction against it? To his thinking, "dwelling" on that horrendous event was not separating them, but was keeping them together. It was Jonathan's own way of invoking the life and presence of Albert. To move on, to act like Albert's passing was insignificant struck Jonathan as a form of abandonment. Jonathan exhaled forcefully. If he was destined to spend the next two billion years thinking of and remembering Albert, then he was prepared to do just such a thing. All he wanted in turn was for the feelings, the sensations, the panic and terror to depart.

When Jonathan became a star again, he wanted to immediately leave the Milky Way, to get away from all the other stars and set out. What he was hoping to do was to travel through the galaxies until he found the white dwarf, the monument commemorating a life now dead. He knew he would recognize it when he saw it.

Turning a corner, he felt a pit in his stomach. He sensed, for the first time, that he was wasting his time here on Earth. What he needed to do was to return to be with the stars, to find that monument. He knew this with confidence.

Still feeling the pit in his stomach, Jonathan walked back to the apartment, lay down on the futon, closed his eyes, and tossed and turned until Blaine came home.

DAY 16

Jonathan Celestial looked at the camera, then at the flower in the distance. He could see Blaine standing next to the camera, tapping his foot restlessly. In the flower Jonathan saw something pure, something beautifully elegant. It was pink, with a yellow center, the petals delicate to the touch. He sighed.

Rob rotated his hat so the bill was facing back. He positioned the camera so it was pointing at Jonathan.

"Should we try again?" he asked.

Blaine said, "Um…yes, that's why we're here."

"Okay! Go for it!"

The music started to play. It was calming, full of rich textures, pearly. Listening to it, to Jonathan, felt like taking a warm bath. Taking Blaine's advice, he let the music "take hold of the heart" as he walked slowly along the grassy field Blaine and his friends created for the set. Feeling the music, Jonathan walked slowly, his bare feet feeling the synthetic grass in his toes. As a guitar figure became prominent in the music he stumbled slightly. He moved across the field, towards the girl who was waiting for him.

"Cut!" Blaine called.

Jonathan turned his head quickly. "What's wrong?"

Blaine walked over and put a hand on Jonathan's shoulder. "You're moving too slowly, too mechanically." He nodded towards Rob, and then turned to face Jonathan. "Give it another go."

Jonathan walked back to where he started. The music was cued, and he moved with all his might, in a quicker, more fluid way.

"Cut!"

Jonathan wondered why Blaine was the one calling cut, but then he remembered that he possessed a distinct vision for the video.

"What's wrong, now?" Jonathan asked.

Blaine walked over. "You're moving too quickly. Try loosening up."

"But—"

"Just give it another try."

Jonathan looked at his feet. "Okay."

Once more the music was playing. Jonathan made his way across the field, mindful of his pace. In a sense, going along this path reminded him of the many trips he made as a star through the deep reaches of space. In the distance was the girl. He kept his eye focused on the flower in the distance. It was drawing him towards it. In that moment, there was nothing to think about except moving towards it. Feeling the fake grass beneath his feet, seeing the flower, he let the music take hold of his heart, though he knew not what that really meant.

It was to his astonishment that he reached the flower without Blaine shouting cut. His mind started to race. Should he bend his knees to pick it up, or rather, bend his back? He did what seemed natural to him. Holding the flower in his hand, he continued on the path before him, looking into the yellow center of the flower, as though it was the source of the music itself.

Now he reached the girl.

Janelle was wearing rainbow-colored dress. She looked at Jonathan, smiling, and proceeded to giggle.

"Cut!"

"I'm sorry," she said, shaking her head. "I just lost it there for a second."

Blaine replied, "Well, you should try to find it." He looked at Jonathan. "Well, at least you're getting your steps in."

Jonathan trotted across the field. He looked up at the blaring lights, putting up a hand to shield his eyes.

Yet again the music played. Jonathan, who now felt like a veteran, went over to the flower, picking it up and soon approaching Janelle. Moving up close to her, he extended the flower towards her. She took it in her hand, and then started laughing.

"Cut!"

"Why are you laughing?" Blaine asked, folding his arms.

"I'm sorry. I don't know. I guess I'm just a little bit nervous, is all."

Blaine put his head in his hand.

"Heard you goofs were filming a flower show in here," a voice called.

Jonathan turned his head and saw that it was Lyla.

Her expression neutral, she walked over to Janelle and Jonathan. "Nice dress," she said.

"Wanna try it on?" Janelle asked.

"What do you mean?" Blaine asked.

Janelle scratched her head. "I don't think this acting business is for me."

"Ooh, I get to act alongside Mr. Weirdo here? Sounds great." Lyla answered.

The two girls ran off. A few minutes passed, and Lyla appeared in the dress. Jonathan's heart was beating quickly.

A new take was started. Jonathan took the flower, approached Lyla, and handed it to her. She held it in her two hands. She kissed the yellow center of the flower. Jonathan watched her lips, his heart still beating rapidly. Then she blew the flower, and the petals scattered across the air. Just as the drums came in, a petal landed in his hand. He looked at it, then at her, just as she was running off. Not sure what was supposed to happen next, he ran after her across the field. The set being small, Lyla soon reached the edge of the synthetic grass. She fell down and lay on the ground, the rainbow hues of her dress waving in the air. Jonathan knelt down beside her. He wrapped his arms around her. He lifted her up off the ground, turning his head towards the blue backdrop, looking at it longingly, the music beginning to fade.

"Cut! That's the one!"

Blaine ran over, waving his arms. "That was perfect! You two…you two have an electrifying chemistry."

Lyla sighed. "Traditional, rigid gender roles aside, I didn't mind being pursued and picked up. Who knew Weirdo here had some strength in him?"

Jonathan put her down. He was breathing heavily. "It all just seemed to flow well." He turned to face Blaine. "Did I walk at the optimal pace?"

"You did. It was all so great."

•••

That night, Jonathan went to bed feeling like a hero. He could hardly wait for Rob to finish editing what was filmed and to see the music video in its full glory. Blaine expressed again and again how excited he was for it to hit the internet and social media.

Not only did Jonathan feel excited, he also felt afraid. Still his heart was racing. He was tossing and turning in his bed. He got up and walked over to the window. Unlatching and opening it, he turned his head skyward to look at the stars. He thought about how so many of them had, for a billion years, been cruel and unkind to him. He clenched his fists.

Hello, Jonathan!

Jonathan knew who it was.

A collection of stars disappeared as a face formed and came into view. Smiling, this was the face of Sir Cosmos, the one who had started the "nice little project" of creating stars.

How are you, Jonathan?

Me? Where do I begin.

From the beginning. Or the middle. Medias res can be refreshingly nice. You could even begin at the end. That could be interesting.

I'll start at the beginning. I came here to Earth to find absolution from my sin, and—

Those are some serious words, Jonathan. What is your sin?

I led Albert into his death. You of all people know that.

Yes, but there is still life to live.

It's my fault! It's my fault that he was destroyed by that supernova.

That may be. But, looking at things from a cosmic perspective, since, well, that's what we do, I think it's important to bear in mind all will be well.

Easy for you to say. You didn't do anything.

Didn't do anything? Jonathan, I've made my fair share of mistakes. But the minute you become too preoccupied with them so as to live for today is the minute you, well, you stop living. How do you expect to find absolution from your sin on earth?

I don't know. I spent so much time watching humans, who live such precious existences. It made me start thinking that I, that I…

You don't even know what you're looking for, Jonathan. No wonder you're halfway through your time off and you feel just as miserable as when you started, if not worse.

Jonathan's jaw was hanging.

Maybe that's the problem.

I think it is, Jonathan. Albert is dead, so he can't forgive you, but he lives on in all of us. What you need to do is to forgive yourself. It comes from within.

Tears were forming in Jonathan's eyes.

Come up here, Jonathan.

I can't.

Like you can't. You're a star; you can float.

Okay.

Jonathan felt his feet leave the ground, as he floated out the window and up, high, into the night sky.

I'm here, Sir Cosmos.

Take a look down, Jonathan.

Below his hovering feet were the tall buildings of downtown Seattle. There were clouds, and there were waters which were like mirrors of ripples. Lights shown in the buildings. The light from the downtown buildings reflected off the water. Jonathan opened his arms, embracing the city in them.

What do you think, Jonathan?

It's…it's amazing. It's incredible.

Take a moment to take it in. All of this is finite, fleeting, and other words that start with "f". My point is, sometimes you need to get high up into the air to see things from a different angle. Albert is gone, that much is true. But that doesn't negate how splendid a view this is. I like to think that anywhere that beautify is to be seen, and rest assured that beauty is everywhere, there, that is where the presence of our loved, lost ones are. I have existed since time immemorial. I have seen many great stars come and go. It is the way of things. I didn't decide on it to be that way, but so it is. What's a cosmic being to do?

I don't know…I feel like I can't let go of that mistake I made all those years ago.

Don't try to let go of it.

What are you trying to teach me?

Sir Cosmos laughed a deep, bellowing laugh. *Who said I was trying to teach you something? I just noticed that it was a lovely night, and I wanted to share that with you. And don't think for a moment I didn't notice the way you look at that girl.*

Janelle?

Not her.

…Lyla?

Yes, that's the one. I can see a spark a million light years away. You really have it for her, don't you?

For Lyla? I…I…I…

Eyes are for seeing. Your time is short on Earth, it's true. But if I were you, I would cherish the time you get to spend with the ones you care about. You can't fix the past. You can create a better future.

What?

Okay, so maybe I AM trying to teach you something, Jonathan. Life is made up of little moments that make it all so wonderful, so spectacular, that…where are the words for it?

Sir Cosmos turned away for a moment.

You better duck, Jonathan. An airplane is coming.

A moment later an aircraft flew between them.

Jonathan floated back up. *With the greatest respect, Sir Cosmos, what are you trying to impart to me?*

Sir Cosmos floated close to Jonathan. *What am I trying to impart to you is not a bunch of words. Words don't do much good. What I am trying to impart to you is an experience. Come on out, boys!*

A group of stars materialized.

Get in formation!

The stars floated around, occasionally bumping into each other. Eventually, they formed none other than the Big Dipper.

Jonathan rubbed his eyes in disbelief.

Come over here, Jonathan.

Jonathan floated towards the Big Dipper. A large celestial spoon, the Big Dipper scooped Jonathan up. Inside, he felt warm water that splashed him in the face. The Big Dipper rocked one way and then other.

Bliss, ecstasy, and an overwhelming joy met Jonathan as he experienced the cosmic bath. Then, as soon as it started, it was over.

The Big Dipper inverted itself, and Jonathan was dumped back into the air, feeling at once the sheer coldness of being wet at such a high altitude.

Sir Cosmos was smiling. *What do you think, Jonathan?*

That…wow.

Now, I know you don't have a lot of time before you come back to being a star, but I want you to try and live every moment with the memory of being in the Big Dipper close to heart. The truth is I believe there is something profound, something wonderful, waiting for you at the end of all this. You just need to focus less on finding some vague notion that doesn't really exist. That, or you need to get a clearer picture of what that notion is. Make it concrete. Make it real. Even if only you believe, if you believe with a full heart then it's real. Either way, do something. Act!

Understood, Sir Cosmos. Thank you.

Day 17

Jonathan Celestial awoke to the sound of the phone ring-ing.

"Hello?" he mumbled, still groggy.

"Hello, Jonathan. This is Bernice. I trust you're well. I am calling on behalf of Agent Gray Willows."

"I remember who you are."

"Excellent. Mr. Celestial, Agent Willows is wondering if you are available for another appointment tomorrow, at noon. Are you available?"

Jonathan gazed at the blank calendar depicting a deer on it hanging on the other side of the room.

"Yes, I can meet with him then."

"Outstanding. Agent Willows will see you then."

"Wonderful." Jonathan put down the phone. "They're out to get me."

Immediately, the phone rang again.

"Hello?"

"Um, yes, is Jonathan Celestial there?"

"Hi, Lyla."

"How's it going?"

"Been better."

"Oh?"

"I don't really feel like going into it."

"Well, okay then. You know, it was a lot of fun being in that music video with you yesterday. I was wondering if you were around tonight, and maybe wanted to grab a drink?"

"A drink?"

"Yes, Weirdo. Alcohol."

"Sure thing. But I tend to go for the coffee."

"Any drinkable liquid will do. I was thinking of The Dolphin. It's a cool spot on Broadway, in Capitol Hill. See you at eight?"

"Sure. See you then."

Jonathan put down the phone. Blaine walked into the room and put a hand at his side:

"Well, aren't you just a chatterbox."

"I'm in trouble, Blaine."

"Yeah? Aren't we all?"

"Agent Willows wants me to come in tomorrow, and Lyla wants me to go out with her tonight." Jonathan was attempting to remember what he learned at the Star Academy. "Is this what you guys call a date?"

Blaine was smiling.

"Is it?" Jonathan asked.

Then Blaine started laughing. "You and Lyla! How did I not see it before?"

"I need help. I thought I didn't know what I was doing two weeks ago. Now? Now, I really don't know what I'm doing."

"Do you like Lyla?"

"At first? No. But I think I am fond of her."

"That wasn't the question."

"What?"

"I asked if you like her? Are you interested in her ro-mantically?"

Jonathan swallowed. "That's a big question."

Blaine poured himself a glass of water. "You certainly had a phenomenal performance together in the music video. That's for sure."

"Blaine?"

"Yes, Jonathan?"

Jonathan's cheeks turned a flushed red and radiated light.

"Jonathan?" Blaine asked. "What's happening to your face?"

Still red, Jonathan said, "I think I might be in love with her."

Blaine set down his glass of water. "What makes you say that?"

"The way I feel when she's around. I feel nervous, and I find that I want to continue to be with her, that I miss her when she's gone."

"Aww, Jonathan!"

"But it can't be!"

"Why not?"

Jonathan looked both ways and then whispered, "Because I'm a star, and in less than two weeks I'm going to return back to space, whether I like it or not. Is that a good reason?"

"Meh, a fling's a fling. Have a little fun. Live a little."

Blaine replied, "Look, Jonathan. I need to get going to work. But you have fun tonight with Lyla. See where things go. Don't get so serious. And as for the interview with the Agent, it is what it is."

"What does that mean?"

"Precisely what the words denote."

"Oh, okay."

"Catch you later."

Jonathan rode the route 49 bus, from the University District to Capitol Hill. He was wearing a white button up shirt and jeans that felt much too tight, all of which came from Blaine. His heart was beating so hard he thought it might come out of his chest. Sweat was forming in his brow. He unfolded the map he obtained from the bus and was able to determine where was best to get off. The bus passed a massive church and Jonathan looked away. The church passed by and was replaced by countless bars. Jonathan looked out the window at the street signs and then walked towards the door of the bus.

"I need to get off here," he told the burly driver.

"Next stop, pal. I'm driving."

"Can't you stop here?"

"I stop where the stops are."

"I don't understand."

The driver stared at Jonathan. "Have a seat," he said.

Eventually, there was a beeping sound, and the driver pointed towards the bus door, now open.

Jonathan got off the bus and walked a block. He saw a sign that showed an arrow and said "Volunteer Park".

Jonathan sighed.

It was a warm evening. The tall buildings of downtown glistened with June sunlight. It seemed that daytime was stretching on indefinitely with the arrival of summer. The streets were crowded with people, many of whom were young and wore colorful clothing.

A neon sign shaped like a dolphin marked Jonathan's destination. He entered, and sat down at the nearest table. For five minutes he sat alone. He looked through the cocktail and beverage menu on the table. All he wanted was a cup of coffee.

"Hey, Weirdo."

He looked up and saw her. Her blonde hair, shoulder-length, and her brown eyes, all of it struck Jonathan in that moment as more beautiful than the most intricate constellation.

"Hi!" Jonathan called.

She sat down. "What are you so peppy about?"

"I was just saying hello. It's a standard custom—"

"You crack me up." She picked up a menu and then put it down right away.

The waitress came by. Lyla ordered a glass of red wine, and Jonathan a cup of coffee.

"You really like coffee, huh?"

"I do! Coffee is a magnificent thing."

"Whatever you say."

"So how was your day?"

"Oh, I helped an old man get a root canal. That was fun."

"Neat."

"What about you? It seemed like something was troubling you when I called."

Jonathan scratched his head, which was feeling hot. "No, no trouble. Nothing is troubling me. I am not troubled."

Lyla stared at him.

Jonathan watched as the waitress brought them their drinks.

"What's going on, Mr. Celestial?"

Jonathan blew on his coffee and smelled it. "Smell is a spectacular, and underrated scent."

"You're trying to distract me. What is it that's bugging you? I may seem prickly, and that's because I am. But know that I do care."

Jonathan leaned in closely towards the table. "I have a friend, who is being investigated."

"Investigated? Ooh! What did he do?"

"Nothing. My friend is completely innocent."

"That's not as fun. I was thinking maybe he stole a lot of money, or pretended to be someone he's not. Know what I mean?"

Jonathan sipped his coffee. "Like I said, he is innocent. But this governmental Agent is pursuing him."

"Well then, Mr. Celestial, I must ask: what is your friend, who by the way is totally not you, accused of having done?"

"My friend is accused of making the crater in Volunteer Park."

Lyla's face lit up. Her smile was beautiful to Jonathan.

"How did your friend do such a thing?"

"He didn't do it. Remember?"

"Okay. So how does the Agent think he did it?"

"They have no evidence on him."

Lyla looked at her drink and said, "Let me get this straight: a friend of yours is accused of making a crater in a park in our own lovely Capitol Hill, but there is no evidence that he did it. Is that correct?"

Jonathan nodded. He felt a pang in his chest.

"Interesting. You remember that I was there the day of all those demonstrations. People are getting really paranoid that there's an alien living among us. It's idiotic. The whole crater thing must just be some sort of meteorological phenomenon. That's all. But that's too bad about your friend, though. Hope justice prevails and he is found innocent." She made a fist in the air as she said this.

"Me too."

"You know, it seems like this whole city has been going a bit crazy ever since that crater. Too bad. I kinda liked the way things were. One thing's for sure: there is change coming on the horizon."

"What do you mean?" Jonathan asked.

"This crater is a big deal. It affects the very psyche of Seattle. People get so much misinformation from so many different places. It seems like the whole situation in Volunteer Park is only making people more divided. It has created a bit of hostility in the air."

"That's too bad."

"Indeed, Jonathan. Too bad. So where do you think the crater came from?"

Jonathan stammered. "It was, er, probably some sort of meteorological event, like you said."

"You're so sweet, agreeing with me and all."

"Well, you are knowledgeable about these things, being a student of astronomy."

Lyla took a sip of her wine. "Correct. I am an expert. I understand that the government, in conjunction with several big scientific agencies, is doing a big investigation behind the crater. My prediction: a couple months will pass with no explanation, and then life will go on. But remember that bit I said about Seattle's psyche? Well the scars that exist there will not heal so quickly. The demonstrations will likely continue. Division will get deeper. I think people are just looking for a witch to burn, even if they have to make one up."

Jonathan replied, "There is no alien, so there is no witch."

Lyla proceeded to laugh. "You are the most precious thing. Like I said, Johnny, change is coming."

They walked out of the bar and into the warm air. On Jonathan's mind was how much he liked being with Lyla. He felt like she brought out the best in him.

"You know I really had a nice time…" Lyla said.

"Yeah? You did?"

She looked at him. "I was parodying how romantic comedies usually play out by saying that. But it is true that I had a nice time. I suppose I really tolerate being around you well. You're just so….so genuine."

"I'm glad you asked me to come out for a drink, Jonathan said."

"Me too. We should do it again sometime soon. That is, if you reciprocally tolerate being around me as much as I you."

"What?"

"If you like me, then let's spend some time together. You know what? I'm not going to call you Weirdo anymore. I'm going to call you,,," she leaned in and kissed him on the cheek. "Jonathan."

Jonathan was glowing red yet again. "I…er….um… well….yes."

Lyla said, "I'll see you later, Jonathan."

"Bye!"

That night, Jonathan opened his book and read eagerly:

Love is a human emotion and phenomenon that binds individuals together, marked by strong affection, and often leads to actions that include procreation.

He felt dissatisfied with what he read. He turned the pages, leafing through the book, thinking of how the study of humans by stars was little more than a spectator sport.

When Lyla kissed him, when her lips touched his cheek, he felt something that set his world on fire. Everything that troubled him, such as the investigation, or the supernova, all of it briefly vanished as he felt the warmth of another's lips against him. For once, he didn't feel alone. He wished she kissed him on the lips. He thought about what it might feel like to kiss her, and it brought a smile to his face.

True, his time was short. So he felt it crucial to make every moment count, and he knew that any moment spent with her was well spent. He lay down on the futon and closed his eyes. Over and over the events of the day played out in his mind like some sort of movie. As he lay there on the futon, he knew he wanted to be with her.

Then thoughts of the next day, of the investigation, came to mind. Somehow, someway, the kiss on his cheek brought him peace and comfort as he anticipated what was to come. Somehow, it made him feel like he would be able to handle whatever came his way.

DAY 18

"It really is a pleasure to meet with you again, Mr. Celestial. Please, have a seat."

Jonathan Celestial sat in the chair, looking out the window of the view of downtown. He could hear the sound of cars passing and honking: the hum of urban life.

Agent Gray Willows gestured with a hand. "How are you?"

"I am fine."

"Let's get right down to business. The lab results on those crystals have not come in, so there is no way for me to know if they are extra-terrestrial in nature, unfortunately."

"I see."

"However," Gray cleared his throat. "Something did happen about a week ago that was rather…peculiar."

"What was that?"

"You see, Jonathan. I heard word from a certain park ranger that a small crater was formed in Cool Waters State Park. I went out to the park. Lovely place. Anyhow, I examined the crater, and its composition, suspiciously, closely resembles that of the one found in our own dear Volunteer Park."

"So?"

"'So'? What I mean to say is that, based on the description of the ranger, it sounds as though you formed the crater in the park. Which leads me to believe that you created the crater here in Seattle."

"Oh," Jonathan had a sip from the glass of water given to him. "Sounds like a case of crater correlation."

"An elegant phrase, Mr. Celestial. What I am beginning to strongly suspect, though I can't quite prove it, is that you are in fact an extra-terrestrial being. Care to confess?"

"Confess to being the alien Seattle is getting so riled up about?"

"Indeed."

Jonathan shook his head. "It's true that I was camping at the park when the crater was formed. The fact of the matter is my friends were being foolish and decided it would be fun to dig a crater, just to mess with folks like you. So they got their shovels, and they dug. The park ranger didn't show up until a bit later. He was a bit clueless, to be honest."

"Well, Mr. Celestial. Your story is all fine and dandy, but the park ranger, and several other campers we talked to, reported hearing a loud crashing sound that day, like an explosion. Surely, your shovels weren't that loud, now were they?"

"I…um…"

"It would appear that the veracity of your testimony is unraveling."

"No it is not. You want the truth? I fell out of a tree, and when I hit the ground, the crater was formed."

"But how did you make it?"

"I don't know. All I did was fall. The same thing happened in Volunteer Park. I am no alien; I just have a tendency to fall from trees."

Gray's expression turned skeptical. "I find it hard to believe that a crater as large as the one in Volunteer Park could possibly be the result of a juvenile suffering gravity." Gray leaned in closely towards Jonathan. "Tell me. You made a crater out in the woods. How did you do it here in Seattle? What's your goal in all of this?"

"Um, to fall less frequently."

Gray leaned back in his chair. "Hilarious! You truly are amusing, Mr. Celestial. Now if you would only tell me the truth."

There was a pause. Jonathan looked at Gray, and saw coldness in his eyes. "Well, it seems that things will have to remain unresolved for right now. I can believe you made the crater at Cool Waters State Park by falling. Volunteer Park? That is a difficult thing for me to believe, Mr. Celestial, a difficult thing, indeed. The crystal labs should be back tomorrow or the next day. If they prove to be not of this world, then I believe I will be ready to write my report and press charges as appropriate. Just know, Mr. Celestial, that in all of this, things are not quite what they seem."

"What do you mean?"

Gray stood up from his seat. "When I investigate a case, I usually start in one place and end up in another. Things are always in motion. Eventually, I reach a conclusion, the truth, which I aim to yield in order to bring about safety for the world. But frequently, things may look one way, only to in fact be another. Take a crystal for example. Held from one angle, it miraculously, splendidly reflects light. Held at a slightly different angle, the display is much different. Appearances can be deceiving. Things, Mr. Celestial, are not quite what they seem."

"I understand what you are saying."

Gray was standing at the window. "Let me tell you a story, Mr. Celestial: When I was younger, just a child, my parents divorced. It was devastating to me and my three siblings. How could two people who had been so in love, who had harbored something so precious, give up on their union? Well, we spent time living with my mother, and then my father. It was unstable to say the least. My mother worked two jobs and was absent much of the time. My father, he did his best, but he had demons of his own. Let's leave it at that. All that to say, I spent most of my childhood, adolescence, and early adulthood not feeling safe or secure, and I vowed that one day I would change that for others, for the world. What I am confronting now is the possibility of an extraterrestrial threat unlike anything the world has ever seen. Do you realize what position this puts me in?"

"I have told you my piece. I have nothing else to share."

"I caught you lying. How can I believe anything you tell me, Mr. Celestial? Trust is not easily earned. Things are not as they seem, but rest assured that the truth will come about in one form or another. For now, you may go."

Walking out of Agent Willows' office, Jonathan heard him speaking softly: "Celestial…you know the name stood out to me from the beginning. But I kept wondering: why would an alien have a name as obvious as 'Celestial'? It seemed like a complete give-away."

DAY 19

"Sounds like you got off easy."

Blaine took a sip of coffee as he said this. The two of them were sitting at the table of the kitchen at the *Eclipse* apartment.

"It sounds like he knows I'm a star; he just can't definitively prove it. That will change once the laboratory report on the crystals come back."

"Which is in a few days, right?"

"Right."

"Well," Blaine folded his hands. "Maybe we will have go on a little trip until things cool down."

Jonathan sipped his coffee. "Things are still tense, aren't they?"

"Oh yeah. I was walking to work the other day, and some more of those groups were demonstrating. It's all over the internet, too."

"The internet! I've heard of that!"

"You just stick to your books. There's nothing good on the internet. Well, except that is how I sell and promote my band's music. So there's that."

Jonathan stood up and walked over to the window. "Where did you learn to play guitar?"

"I taught myself."

"You are awfully skilled at that apparatus."

"Remember what I said? It's an 'instrument'."

"Yes, you are skilled at manipulating it."

"'Playing' it."

"Oh, okay!"

"Yes, I learned when I was in high school. As you might guess, I was really into post-rock bands at that time. I...I had a lot of feelings going through my teenage brain, and I found a release in that form of music. You see, just as I was starting high school, my parents divorced. My mom was having an affair. Anyway, it was a really nasty divorce, full of lawyers and paperwork. I wouldn't wish that fate on anyone."

"I read about divorces and familial stability in my book."

"I bet you did. Well, we didn't have a lot of familial stability. It was really hard, going through that divorce. Here I was, a fourteen-year-old kid getting ready for high school. All I wanted was to get decent grades and talk to cute girls, and then all of a sudden my center was being pulled out from under me. Always I had felt closer to my dad. I remembered learning to ride a bike and fish from him. But I was close to my mom, too. It felt like suddenly I had to choose sides, and I didn't want to do that. I remember my parents talking to each other, the way they would whisper in harsh tones, or occasionally yell. Sometimes, they wouldn't even talk at all. That was probably the worst thing, the silent dinners."

"What was the outcome of that pivotal event?"

"The divorce? Well, my little sister and I had to spend time between the two parents. I would spend one week with my dad, and then a week with my mom. It felt so weird. It was so fragmented. It definitely brought my sister and I closer together. We had to look out for each other, you know? I remember reassuring her, telling her that everything was going to be okay, when I full well had no idea if things were going to be that way."

"That sounds hard."

"You can say that again. Going to school was tough. I remember struggling with fitting in. I was so mad! I got involved in photography. I would go down to the beach and take pictures of the water meeting the shore. Somehow that comforted me. It made me think of the idea that the pieces of my life, which were fragmented, were coming back together, the idea that the water was smoothing the sand over and bringing restoration."

"Water is a mesmerizing phenomenon. I can't think of another planet that has it."

"For a long time I was angry. I was bitter and spiteful. I had no interest in God or any sort of higher power, but I was always drawn to music. So my friend Rob got me into post-rock, which was bombastic and cinematic and emotional. I connected with it in a profound way, I guess. For Christmas Sophomore year I asked my dad for a guitar, amp, and a basic pedal board. He didn't get me any of that, but when we celebrated Christmas with my mom later that day I got exactly what I had asked for."

"Oh, neat!"

"So I worked hard, playing around with different sounds and effects. I was always drawn to textures, to the ways in which sound could embody feelings. That was what interested me. I was involved at school, playing on the soccer team and even singing in the choir. I guess I have always been a pretty musical dude. Eventually I met the guys who would be my band mates- well, that was my first band. At the request of our singer, we played covers of indie pop bands. It was fun, but I wanted to write songs. It turned out that Mitch and I went to the same college. We met Tim at UW, and so Static Sea was born. We played around on campus and at local coffee shops. It was a lot of fun."

"I bet!"

"You see, commercial success has never been my goal; I just like making music. I was happy to be playing, plain and simple. We recorded a few CD's, and I think it's safe to say we got better with each subsequent work. A few EP's later, and we were working on our debut album. You came along just after we finished our second album."

"I have had time to listen to your album. I must say it is a fantastic experience."

"Thank you! We worked hard on it, and I was anxious all throughout the mixing and mastering process."

"I see."

"But anyway. What I am realizing I haven't told you a lot about myself. This is what I want you to walk away with: I'm a barista who is in a band, which makes me like sixty-thousand other people in Seattle. But I don't worry about making it big like other bands. I'm happy with how we are. I'm just happy to be able to make music. It brings me joy. You should find something creative to do for fun."

"I should!"

"But like I was saying earlier, life hasn't always been easy for me. When I went off to college I kept in touch with my dad, but I sorta stopped talking to my mom. It wasn't that I hated her or anything. It's just that I never really regained trust in her again after I found out about her cheating. It was like a piece of her was missing, that my sister and I couldn't access her. She wasn't available."

"So you severed your familial ties?"

"Well, I suppose that is what I did. It felt like she made the decision for us. In college, she occasionally wrote letters, but I didn't really hear from her."

"Did you write letters in response?"

"Sometimes. Sometimes, she called too. But it always felt so weird talking to her. I hated it. It made me hate myself, too, for how I was acting towards her. I was cold and distant. Looking back on what happened, I feel a bitterness, I feel hurt, and I can't say that it has fully healed. I struggle with trusting people. When I first met you, I thought you were the weirdest person I had ever met."

"Weird?"

"Weird doesn't cover it. You're bizarre. I thought you were a psycho. But with time I can say I've really grown to like you. Especially when you told me the story of the supernova, I realized that, really, you and I aren't so different. We both carry scars with us. I guess that's why I was drawn to you, and felt happy looking after you."

"That would explain why you were willing to let me lodge with you."

"Yes, it would. Anyway, to summarize. I couldn't care less if the band ever makes it big. Like I said, I'm content to play house shows and just record music. Right now, lately, I have been more focused on your wellbeing, which is refreshing. It is refreshing to be worried about another person, and not caught up solely in the world of your own thoughts. You should give it a try sometime, I mean, maybe when you make it back up to the world of the stars."

They heard the sound of voices from outside the window of the *Eclipse* apartment.

Blaine turned to look at Jonathan. "What's that sound outside?"

"Let's go find out."

They walked outside. Blaine said, "I don't see anything."

Jonathan was pointing at the sky. "There, that's what everyone must be talking about."

In the sky, the moon was passing between the sun and the earth, forming a solar eclipse. A deep black circle, but with a radiant cusp of light around the edges, the eclipse was incredible.

"Best not to look at it with the naked eye," Blaine said.

They turned away.

Jonathan closed his eyes.

Hey, Moon.

Jonathan.

How are you?

Nothing is going my way.

I'm doing pretty good. What are you doing?

Oh, just passing through. I try to make a round every once in a while, at least once a day. Not that there's any point to it all.

It sure is a great display

Thanks, I guess. How are things on Earth?

You know, it's all right.

The Star Keeper misses seeing you around. Says things aren't the same.

Things will never be the same, Moon. I need to go. Keep up the great work.

Okay, Jonathan.

Jonathan turned towards Blaine, who appeared indignant "You keep talking to celestial bodies like that, and the demonstrators will find you in no time."

"Eclipses are amazing things. 2-4 of them happen on Earth annually."

"Were you talking to the moon?"

Jonathan answered, "Yes!"

"Here, let's head back inside."

Seated in the kitchen, Blaine said, "I suppose eclipses are kind of like life itself. They are beautiful, fleeting, and infrequent. It's best to appreciate them for what they are."

"Yes," Jonathan answered, "to embrace them, to embrace eclipses and life. That is a good thing to do. I can't say how hard it was for your parental units to divorce, but it's still worth it to embrace life. It's still worth it."

"I'm gonna have to wrestle with that one." Blaine was not meeting Jonathan's eyes. Then he turned to look at him and said, "Say, how about we go see if we can't find a good cup of coffee?"

Jonathan's eyes glowed. "Sounds amazing! Let's go."

They rose from the table, and walked towards the door. They went outside, got on a bus, and were off through the city.

Day 20

Jonathan Celestial was walking towards the coffee machine when he heard the phone ringing. Something felt different today to him, as though there was a calm silence that the ringing phone punctured.

"Hello?"

"Hello, Mr. Celestial." It was Gray Willows.

"How may I be of service to you today?"

"I would like you to come down to my office as soon as possible."

"As soon as—"

But the phone dial tone was all that could be heard. Jonathan looked around the apartment, and then remembered that Blaine was at work. He smacked the kitchen table with a clenched fist, letting loose a deep sigh.

•••

"Hello, Mr. Celestial. Please, follow me."

They walked through the long corridor towards his office.

Jonathan sat down in the chair.

"I received the results from the crystal labs."

"Okay."

"And I have finished writing my report on the crater in Volunteer Park."

"What is the outcome? What is the truth you arrived at?"

Gray walked around the desk towards Jonathan. "You're far too eager to hear the truth, Mr. Celestial."

Jonathan glared at him, feeling bold. "Just tell me what you brought me all the way down here to learn."

Gray stood still. He smiled. "Those crystals are not of this world. You, Mr. Celestial, are an extra-terrestrial."

Jonathan was no longer thinking. "You have no way to prove it."

"Oh, a classic answer. Mr. Celestial, I was nothing if not methodical. I was scrupulous. I was—"

"Way too wordy."

"Don't you dare talk to me like that! Mr. Celestial, don't you know I can use the full power of the law on you?"

"Okay you want to know the truth?" Jonathan asked. "The truth is, I'm a star, who came to Earth. That's it."

"I know, Mr. Celestial."

"And if you don't mind, I think I will be leaving now."

Gray sat down at his desk. He pressed a switch next to his coffee mug. A clicking sound followed.

Jonathan pulled on the door handle, but it didn't budge. Jonathan looked at Gray, who was smirking.

"What in the world—"

A second clicking sound followed, and the floor beneath Jonathan's feet retracted. He fell down a chute, landing in a cell with barred walls.

Jonathan looked around. He called out for help, his voice reverberating throughout the room. All was silent.

A few minutes later and the only door in the room opened as Gray entered and then closed. He was breathing heavily.

"I tell you, these stairs, even going down, do a number on my knees."

"What are you doing to me? I'm innocent. All I did was be a star."

Gray Willows looked behind him, as though he was checking that the door was closed:

"So you say you're a star. Well, I have some news for you, Mr. Celestial." He reached out a hand. His fingers glowed in a luminous display. "I too, am a star. I have spent a long time searching for you. I have traveled throughout space, looking for you, with one simple purpose."

"Which is?"

Gray extended his other hand, and a beam of energy shot out of it, striking Jonathan. He groaned in pain, shrinking back, then falling over. On the ground, he continued to shake.

"My purpose is to make you suffer as much as I have, Jonathan. It took me a while, because I had to stage a plausible investigation before I could apprehend you, but the time has now come for justice to take place." He looked at Jonathan with eyes that were full of spite. "My name is Albert Bright."

•••

The waves of energy rocked Albert Bright in one direction and then another. Utterly at the mercy of the supernova, Albert was blasted by colorful light that was unfurling like a flower. He was tossed through space until he was in a distant galaxy. For a little while, several hundred million years, Albert was dim, unaware of anything. Eventually, he opened his eyes, only to find that his luminosity was not what it used to be. His energy was depleted, and he felt as though he was beyond being a white dwarf, that he was living in some sort of monstrous nightmare.

There was only one emotion that Albert felt in that moment: a consuming rage, like a fire that could not be quenched. He knew that he had to do whatever was necessary to return to the Milky Way, to find Jonathan, and to make him feel precisely what Albert was now feeling: a pain beyond words.

Disoriented, Albert floated through the dark reaches of space, looking for anything that might indicate where he was. But all there was, as far as he could see, was pure darkness, a form of oblivion.

The anger would not fade. He moaned, the pain overwhelming. On and on he floated. There was only one object that he was thinking of: he needed to find Jonathan.

"If he had listened to me…if he had listened to me," he whispered.

A few million years of wandering and Albert came upon a space filled with white dwarves. The sign of a dead star, the white dwarf was a haunting figure that silenced all stars. For as far as Albert could see, there were white dwarves. By his estimation, he had only just barely avoided becoming just such a being. Albert thought that he wanted Jonathan to be one of these, but he suspected that there was an even worse fate for his former-friend, to live and be in unbearable pain, to live and wish for death, but to be unable to have that release.

So Albert continued to travel. Eventually, far off in the distance, he saw a black hole. Sucking up light at a rapid pace, this was a cosmic force of pure destruction. Having no need to learn lessons, Albert kept his distance, admiring the black hole in its deadly splendor. Truly, there was nothing that could escape its pull. Albert initially thought being sucked into a black hole might be an appropriate consequence for Jonathan, but it would be too quick, and it would bring about death rather than perpetual suffering.

There was a moment when he felt the tugging sensation, thinking that he was being pulled in by the black hole. Using the last of his energy, he soared out of the reach of its pull. He felt an awe for this cosmic force, but with that awe there was an accompanying fear.

Several hundred million years of wandering followed. Only occasionally was there another star. He tried talking to them, but many of them turned to look away from Albert, who had been disfigured so grotesquely by the supernova. None of them knew the way back to the Milky Way. It appeared as though he would never make it back.

The loneliness gnawed at him.

Often, he needed to stop to try and regain his strength. There was little relief, for when he stopped moving he became aware of how much pain he was in. He imagined Jonathan, that star who always beamed with such brightness. All he felt for him was hatred. He envisioned the brightness of Jonathan Celestial, and then he imagined all going dark for him.

Finally, after millions of years of traveling, of struggling just to stay in motion, Albert returned to the outskirts of the Milky Way, and it was here that he began to live in secrecy. He stayed out of the reach all stars. Only Sir Cosmos, who tended to know most things, was aware of Albert's presence.

"I can see you are hurting, Albert. How can I help?" he asked him.

"Leave me alone, old man. I have no need for you or anyone."

Sir Cosmos sighed. "I know you plan to seek revenge on Jonathan. Just know that what you are seeking, by the means with which you are seeking it, is unattainable."

"Did you not hear me? I said I have no need for you, or for anyone for that matter. I know what I am going to do, and you can't stop me."

"Do what you must. All experiences are educational, especially the bad ones, so go ahead."

Albert learned from eavesdropping on stars that Jonathan Celestial was planning to use his PTO, once he had a sizable sum, to travel to Earth, to search for something, a peace from the guilt and remorse he felt. From watching Jonathan in secret Albert was able to surmise that he was sorry for what happened, haunted by it even. But that didn't matter to Albert. What Jonathan needed, he thought, was to feel what Albert felt. Keeping a close eye on Jonathan, always in secret, Albert began to gradually formulate a plan.

The moment Jonathan traveled to Earth and started his vacation, Albert followed closely behind. Having done research into the Bureau of Astral Anomalies, Albert was aware of an Agent named Gray Willows. Unlike Jonathan, who formed a crater in the middle of a park, Albert was more tactful, landing gracefully on the surface of the Earth with no impact. Immediately Albert found Gray Willows. He cornered him in his office, reached out a hand, and at once took on the appearance of Gray. Then, he took Gray and tied him up, placing him in the closet, promising to provide him with food and not harm him. After all, Gray had not wronged Albert.

Observing the crater, it was then that Albert, or Gray rather, began his investigation.

DAY 21

As dark and empty as space itself, Jonathan Celestial awoke to find himself still in a holding cell. He reached out his hands to touch the bars before him. He turned to see the other three walls. He looked up and saw the high ceiling. Escape, it seemed, was impossible.

Jonathan sat down. Tears fell from his eyes. He had tried his hardest do good, to be good, but all that had been wrought was hurt and darkness. Then he noticed that there was a window on the wall, located high up. The bars that ran along the window were titanium. In a fury Jonathan grabbed the bars of the cell and punched them.

"Hold it right there!"

A guard approached Jonathan. He pulled out a taser and pointed it at him.

"One more move," the guard said, "and you're going back to sleep."

"I didn't mean anything…" Jonathan had his hands raised in the air as he stepped back towards the wall.

"There," the guard said, "That's what I thought."

Sitting in the corner of the cell, Jonathan began thinking. What was Lyla doing at this particular moment? Surely she was working on her research? What about Blaine? How was Static Sea doing? Then there had been his acting career. Would he ever again perform for others?

Holding his hands in his head, he stared through the bars at the guard, who was seated, looking right back at him, watching his every movement Looking up, Jonathan could see that there was an air vent. He could easily float into the air and crawl through. But doing so would alert the guard, who doubtlessly would send the others to apprehend him. What he needed was to figure out a way to distract the guard, to buy some time to escape, without the guard knowing how he did it.

Jonathan stood and looked out the window. It was getting dark out. No stars were visible, but there was the moon. At once Jonathan was seized by an idea.

He closed his eyes and called out to his old friend, the moon:

Hello?

Jonathan.

How are you?

Not great.

Why?

Because I continue to try to bring light to unfathomable darkness. What about you?

Long story. As you know, I have been living as a human, but now I have been locked up by an Agent who is actually Albert. All I want to do is be a human, to experience what that means, to find a way to be set free from my past. Now it looks like my past, present and future are more connected than I thought.

Huh?

The Agent who has been pursing me is the person I have been longing to be forgiven by. The truth is I am still processing it all. It's gonna take me a while to wrap my head around things. Maybe a few million years.

Whoa.

Anyway, I need to call in a favor.

What, Jonathan?

Can you shine down some lunar rays, something to get that guard's attention.

Where is he? I can't see him.

He's seated on the other side of these bars.

Is there a window over there?

Yes.

Okay, I will shine down some lunar rays on him, but moving over there may affect the tides. I'm not too sure how the Southern Hemisphere will do.

That's okay.
Okay, here I go.
Thanks, moon.
Okay, Jonathan. Just remember that none of this matters, any-way.

After Jonathan opened his eyes, he noticed that nothing had changed. Then, from the window behind the guard, a dazzling, mesmerizing amber light poured into the room, filling it awash with soft radiance.

The guard, panicking, looked around him. "What in the — what are you doing? I'll shock you for this!"

Jonathan wore an innocent expression. "I don't know what is happening. I'm scared."

The guard turned around and looked through the window, out at the moon. "It's the moon," he said. It was then that the hypnotic, potent effect of the moon's light happened. The guard, so mesmerized by the lunar rays, was unable to look away from the moon.

"So beautiful…so pretty."

This was Jonathan's chance. He gently hovered into the air, removing the lid from the air vent, and proceeded to climb through. The lunar rays would last approximately two minutes. This, he hoped, should give him enough time to make an escape.

Jonathan navigated his way through the vent, taking a turn to the left and then to the right. He tried to be quiet, but he knew he was making a lot of noise. Eventually he reached another opening below. He looked, seeing that it was Gray Willow's office. The Agent was pacing, occasionally sitting at his table to look over the papers stacked on his desk. Jonathan continued shuffling through the vent. He reached a point where he had to climb upward through the vent. The darkness frightened him, so he illuminated a finger as a sort of flashlight. He climbed up, making a horrible amount of noise. Then he found himself crawling above another opening. He looked down and saw that there was a door and windows.

Hey, Moon!

Yes?.

A little help!

One second. Oof. All this moving around. I don't move as well as I used to, you know.

Once more rays of resplendent lunar light filled the space below the vent. The guards on duty were mesmer-ized, wandering over to the windows to look at the moon. Jonathan, feeling emboldened, kicked the vent latch, and fell onto the ground. The two guards were too occupied with looking at the moon to notice that he had escaped. He walked over to the door, opened it, and stepped out into the night air. He immediately ran across the street. Looking up, he saw that the moon was close, emanating pure light onto the city. Such a sight was lovely to behold. But Jonathan could not stay still. He ran up the slope and found his way, eventually, back to his apartment.

DAY 22

"No way, Jonathan…"

Jonathan Celestial scratched his eyes and said to Blaine, "It's the truth. The Agent and Albert are one!"

Blaine put down his mug of coffee. "Are you sure?"

"He told me the story of how he survived the supernova and came to Earth. Everything adds up. I have no choice but to believe him."

"So what do we do then?"

"I don't know, but it's only a matter of time before Albert finds me. He said he wanted me to suffer as much as he had. It was scary!"

"I bet." Blaine put a copy of the newspaper on the table. "Check this out. More bad news."

Jonathan held the newspaper in his hands and took a closer look:

Who is Jonathan Celestial?
A Seattle Messenger Special Report

Note: this piece is a companion to a prior report concerning the formation of a crater in Volunteer Park.

Some say he is an alien.

Others? A psycho.
One thing's for sure: he's a mystery.

SEATTLE-Yesterday, it was revealed by the Bureau of Astral Anomalies that a being with connections to outer space itself has been living among the citizenry of Seattle for close to three weeks. While being held for testing and research, Celestial, as he refers to himself, escaped.

"At this moment, I cannot comment on the nature of this being," Agent Gray Willows said during an emergency press conference. "What I can say is that he has access to resources that are extraterrestrial in nature, including celestial crystals. Further, we have reason to believe that he can manipulate the trajectory and luminescence of the moon. One thing is for sure, that he is an imminent threat to the safety of our society."

Willows was not able to disclose any further details, other than that the city is cooperating with the Bureau to search for him. A picture of Celestial is included with this piece. If you or someone you know sees someone who strongly resembles the individual depicted, then please call the following number:

1-888-CELESTI

"We don't want the public to panic," Willows said. "But it is important to know that this guy has powers we have never seen the likes of. Standard safety precautions are recommended. If we work together, we can catch this guy."

Jonathan threw the newspaper on the floor. His voice shaking, he said, "Blaine, I'm scared."

"You don't need to be scared, Jonathan. It's a scary situation, but I know that you will prevail."

"Easy for you to say. You don't have a planet coming after you."

"Me? No, no more than usual."

Jonathan sighed.

Blaine said, "But don't you think this means you can get what you came to Earth for? Doesn't this mean you can obtain forgiveness from Albert?"

Jonathan looked intently into Blaine's eyes. "When I learned that Gray was Albert, I didn't see any sign of my friend in him. He has changed. Whoever I knew as my friend is gone."

Blaine leaned over towards Jonathan. "You know, it has always been my belief that, though friends may change throughout life, their core essence never does. Albert may be impersonating a governmental Agent and be on a revenge mission, but he is still Albert. Really."

"Easy for you to say. And what's the deal with the phone number listed in the article. Is it Polish?"

"It has to be 7 digits, Jonathan."

"They cut my name short!"

Blaine rose from his seat at the kitchen table. "There's no telling how all of this is going to affect the city. Things could get ugly." Blaine turned and looked at Jonathan, his expression brightened. "I have an idea. It's a little…out there, but then again, so are you."

"What's your idea?"

Blaine placed both his hands on the table. "I think we need to escape for a little while. I have some time off accrued at work. You're not the only one with PTO. Well, I don't get paid for it, but that's beside the point. Listen, I say we head to the peninsula and lay low for a little bit."

"Do I have a choice in any of this?"

Blaine laughed. "Take a look out the window, but be careful."

Poking his head through the window, Jonathan saw that a crowd was gathering in the street below. People were yelling and chanting. Jonathan could hear the sound of a helicopter flying overhead.

Jonathan turned to look at Blaine. "I don't think I have much of an option."

Blaine went from the *Eclipse* apartment to the car, loading it with camping supplies. Rob, Mitch, and Tim all came over to the apartment. Blaine filled them in on

Jonathan's true identity and had them swear an oath of secrecy, which they did gladly. They then got in the car and waited for a clearing in the marching crowd so Blaine could back out of the parking garage. They waited for a long while.

Jonathan was lying down on the floor in the back of the car. "What is the peninsula like?" he asked.

Blaine was looking both ways as people continued to walk by. "It's a far-off and magical place."

"Neat!"

Eventually they were able to pull out of the garage and made it to 45th street.

Soon they were speeding along I-5, swiftly, heading south.

Now that they were out of the city, it was safe for Jonathan to sit up in the car. Rob was trying to teach him how to play solitaire.

"I don't get it," Jonathan said. "The cards alternate in color. Shouldn't they all match?"

"I didn't make the rules; that's just the way it is."

Card by card they were making their way through the game. Occasionally Jonathan drew a card from the stack.

Rob turned his hat backwards. "You have to do it in 3's."

"What?"

Rob drew three cards and showed Jonathan.

"But why can't I just draw a single card? This game is ludicrous."

"You wanted to learn."

"Yes I did. I love learning!"

So they continued to play. Soon, Jonathan was playing by himself, with little guidance from his friend. But unfortunately, it came to pass that Jonathan lost.

"There are no moves afforded me," Jonathan said.

"Yes, I'm afraid you lost."

"Lamentable!"

"People lose most of the time."

"But still hope remains of winning," Jonathan said, smiling.

Blaine was driving in the middle of five lanes. Deciding that it would be prudent to merge as a way to speed up, he put on his turn signal. Just as he was merging left, so too was a car on the other side merging right into the same lane. Nearly scraping the car, he turned back, the car jerking. Everyone was quiet. The car continued to jerk, and Blaine nearly went into the other lane. Behind, they heard the sound of cars colliding. Blaine slowed down to a much gentler pace, waiting for the car to stabilize after all the movement.

"What in the world?" Mitch cried.

"I'm not familiar with that sort of driving," Jonathan said, "that was frightening."

"Is everyone okay?" Blaine asked.

Rob said, "What the heck are you doing, Blaine?"

"I was just trying—"

"You could have killed us all!"

It was in that moment that Jonathan Celestial realized the fragility of human life.

"So suddenly…it can all end, just like that." Jonathan tried to snap his fingers, but there was no sound.

"It's true, Blaine said."

"We go about our lives, doing the things we do, eating, walking, working, and then it all ends."

"Right."

"For stars, it's a very gradual process. We have an elaborate ceremony to celebrate the starhood of a comrade before he or she fades off. But you humans? It's chaos!"

"That doesn't even cover all the other ways you can go. A car accident is one way to die, but don't forget disease, war, accidents of all sorts, and the many other ways."

"The sensations I was feeling just a minute ago were frightful. Heart pounding, pain in my chest. It felt as though time came to a halt!"

Blaine looked in the mirror and said, "Guys, I'm so sorry…I don't know what to say. If any of you were hurt, I don't know how I would have been able to live with myself."

"Welcome to my world," Jonathan said. "I was always nervous about becoming a white dwarf, but the idea of dying as a human is much worse."

"It can be scary," Rob admitted.

"Fear can be a common reaction," Blaine said, "but I don't think it is necessary, or helpful, really."

Jonathan said, "Fear! What an emotion. It grips the entire body!"

Rob said, "I have always been afraid of death, but I do find comfort in my faith."

"Tell me more."

"Well, as a Christian, I find peace in knowing that when I die I will be with God forever. He even tells us to not fear."

"That sounds comforting," Jonathan said. "I find comfort in the fact that Sir Cosmos tells us to never fear."

"What are you talking about?" Blaine asked.

"I saw him, Sir Cosmos, the other night."

"Is that God?"

"No, but he was the one who came up with the idea of having stars light up the night sky. Not even he knows how he was created."

"Interesting…" Blaine muttered.

"Tell me," Jonathan said, "what does it mean to be with your God forever?"

Rob paused. "I have thought about this a lot. Eternity scares me a bit. It just seems like a long time!"

"We stars can live for billions of years. So maybe it's like living a billion years, and then another billion years, and then another billion years, and then—"

"That won't work," Blaine interjected. "You're dealing in the finite, however large the pieces are. What Rob here is talking about is the infinite, something that humans fundamentally can't understand."

"Oh?"

"To me," Blaine continued, "Life is life. When it ends, there is nothing more. As I've said, consciousness ceases. There is no need for the next thing, for an afterlife."

"Afterlife…is that what comes after life?"

"Yes, precisely."

Jonathan said, "Life is so wonderful and amazing and incredible. A billion years might sound like a long time to you humans, who are lucky to live a hundred years, but boy, do they go by fast!"

"Time is funny like that," Blaine said. "Time is what it is. Life comes, life goes."

"It still scares me," Rob said. "You know, I've always been an anxious person. God promises me eternal life with him, but I am prone to fear."

Jonathan asked, "What are you anxious about?"

Rob crossed his left leg over his right. "It isn't that I'm anxious about any one thing. I just feel this dread a lot of the time, that something bad is going to happen. I fear getting sick and dying, or getting in a car accident, as you just nearly experienced. I get scared!"

"Being scared is horrible!"

"You two," Blaine said, "there is no need for fear. All things in the universe will correct themselves. Or, as you might put it, Rob, God will look out for you. You are safe."

Rob said boldly, "I can't help the way I feel, now can I? I have clinical anxiety."

"What does that mean?" Jonathan asked.

Blaine said, "Let Rob explain himself."

Rob said, "Thank you. Anxiety, as I understand it, is different for everyone. But it is a diagnosable phenomenon."

"Diagnosable?"

"Yes," Rob continued. "Anxiety is a mental health condition. It affects millions of people. It has physical symptoms, like chest pain or sweaty palms, and it also has emotions, like panic and fear, along with thinking that centers on bad things happening. To summarize, in a broad sense, it is a lot of things: a set of physical sensations, emotions, and thought patterns."

"Sounds intricate," Jonathan said, "and interesting! But also scary. You know, I think I have had some of those symptoms myself."

"It is scary. So many people around the world suffer from it, or depression, but each and every single person, for the most part, thinks that they are suffering alone."

"Why is that?"

"Because," Blaine said, "the reality, or the illusion, rather, is that we are all trapped inside of our own heads, and that that is all there is."

"I'm confused," Jonathan said.

"Don't worry about it," Rob replied. "All I want to get across is that many people, myself included, are anxious. And you know what? That's okay. I've got God looking out for me, and great friends like you all."

"Such a kind sentiment!" Jonathan declared. "I like what you two are saying about us all being connected. As a star, when I look at the Earth, I can see it all. Well, often Asia is on one side and North America the other. But my point is that I can see the…um…"

"Totality?" Blaine suggested.

"Yes! I can see the totality of humanity, and I realize that you all really are in it together."

"In what?"

"Engaged in the experience of living life," Jonathan said.

"That, too, is comforting Rob said. But it doesn't' stop me from having my anxious moments."

"Life can be scary! But that's sort of part of what makes it, well, life, isn't it?" Jonathan said.

"Sure is," Blaine replied.

Jonathan said, "We could all die in a horrible car accident at any moment, and that would be it. What happens next? One of you says eternal life with God, while the other says there is a whole lot of nothing. But what even happens if there is truly nothing after this?"

"What do you mean?" Blaine asked. "There's nothing, and then nothing, and then still more nothing."

"But what you are describing sounds like something," Jonathan challenged.

"You two are getting way too cerebral for me," Rob said. "All I know is that I want to strive to trust in God, to live life for and with him, to love Him and my neighbor as myself."

"Beautiful!" Jonathan proclaimed. "What does that mean, to love a neighbor as yourself?"

"Well, let's break it down," Blaine said. "Your neighbor is whoever you are near."

Rob added, "It doesn't matter who that person might be. Religion, race, sexual orientation, etc. it doesn't matter, you need to love them in the same way that you love yourself."

"Beautiful!" Jonathan repeated.

"Yes," Blaine said, "this stuff is simple in the abstract, but it can get much trickier in practice."

"You know, I was angry when I was in a Christian church. I read in the sacred text about how dwelling on past mistakes prevents love from flourishing, or something like that."

"Sounds about right," Blaine answered.

"Anyway, I was really angry, because it felt like the entire religion at large was condemning me for how I was living."

"Welcome to religion."

"It's actually a bit more complicated if you look a bit deeper," Rob said.

"I'm sure it is," Jonathan replied. "I'm just expressing how I felt in the moment. Anyway, I think religion, like my book, helps to provide answers to important questions for people. I know that I have a lot more questions now than I did when I started my time here on Earth."

"Interesting," Blaine replied.

"That's the truth," Jonathan said. "Anyway, when I decided I wanted to come down to Earth, they warned me. They told me there was a host of problems here. The Star Keeper explained it some more for me. He told me that life here was difficult and challenging, and that it was not the best way to use PTO. But still I felt that something special was here. I just knew it!"

"And you know what?" Blaine asked. "I'm inclined to think you will find it."

Jonathan let his head hang low. "The only thing I've encountered here, other than you all and Lyla—"

"So what's the story there?" Blaine asked.

"What do you mean?"

"You met with her for coffee a few days ago. You told me you thought you were in love with her. Are you in a relationship?"

"My relationship with her is quite amicable. Thank you for asking."

"Come on, Jonathan!" Blaine said. "It's obvious she is nuts about you. Are you nuts about her?"

"I am terribly fond of her."

The car was quiet for a moment.

"Okay! I love her! I think she is the is the most wonderful thing. However, it can't last. Soon I will have to return to my post as a star, and she will continue on with her life." Jonathan sighed. "We can't be together."

Blaine looked in the mirror at Jonathan for a brief moment. "That's tough."

Rob turned his hat back around again. "I think…as far as the best way to go about it is…you will need to do some reflection."

"Don't you think I am doing that already?"

"Yes…well—"

"I wish I could just stay here on Earth. But it turns out the star who I thought was my best friend is now trying to hunt me down and make me suffer." Jonathan hit the car seat with his fist. "As if I haven't already suffered."

"Which is why we are getting away for a little while. This will allow us to process and come up with a plan for how to best proceed, both when it comes to Lyla as well as Albert."

"Thanks, Blaine."

Blaine handed Jonathan a pair of sunglasses. "So try and look at things a little lighter. For being a star, you can get awfully heavy about things. There may be some challenges, but hey, you're here, you're alive, you're with us."

"True enough."

They continued to drive. They arrived at Olympic National Park later that night.

DAY 23

Please, Albert…

No, Jonathan. I will not do that.

Why not?

…

Why not?!

I shouldn't even have to answer something as stupid as that.

Well, I need you to answer. I don't care if it makes me stupid. I just want to make things right.

You want to make things right? Well, isn't that great! Do you have any idea what I went through, how many years I suffered, just so I could get to this moment and have you ask for me to forgive you? I don't forgive you. I don't forgive you, and I never will. You want to make things right? Then you're going to have to pay the price.

Albert—

•••

Waking up in a cold sweat, breathing heavily, Jonathan Celestial looked up at the ceiling of the tent. He could hear the sound of crickets. Everyone else appeared to be asleep. He spent a few minutes lying there, hoping to drift back off to sleep. But, as seemed to be the norm lately, sleep was eluding him. He moved towards the door of the tent. It took him a moment to unzip the flap; he was still trying to figure out how zippers worked, but then he got it.

Jonathan made his way along a wooded path towards a hill. He went up the hill, and as he reached the top, he noticed that Comrade Sun was rising. As light spread, he was able to see a panoramic view of trees as far as the eye could see. Such a view was breathtaking. There were mountains, rivers, and collections of trees everywhere. All was splashed with shades of green and blue.

Comrade Sun.

Jonathan! How are you, buddy?

Not great.

That's too bad. Sir Cosmos was telling me about Albert.

Yes. It's a very…delicate situation, Sun. I don't know what to do. I can't sleep. I can't think.

Jonathan, I want to remind you of something. Do you remember what I showed you when you first got to Earth?

What?

You were searching for a home, for a sense of belonging. Jonathan, when you were standing down by the water, by Pike Place, I shone some light on the Olympic Mountains, creating a dazzling display if I may say so myself. Guess what. Now you ARE in the Olympic Mountains! How neat is that? Here, let me shed some light on the situation.

Warm, resplendent sunlight emanated from Comrade Sun, reflecting off the waters and the tips of the mountains. Everything around Jonathan was glowing with precious light.

Remember, Jonathan. Nothing brightens a day like… brightness!

Of course.

So things may seem tough right now. But sometimes, looking at things just a little differently can make things better. Know what I mean?

I do. Thank you, Comrade Sun.

Anytime. Well, in particular, find me during sunrise and sunset for the best results.

Encouraged, Jonathan walked down the hill towards the camping area. Blaine was seated at the picnic table.

"What are we going to do today?" Jonathan asked with excitement.

"Oh, hey there. Today we are going to go on a hike. Clear our heads a little. Then tonight, we're going to chat around the fire."

"Sound serious."

"It really isn't. What are you smiling about?"

"I just talked to Comrade Sun. He's one of the few stars who will still talk to me."

"Who wouldn't want to talk to you?"

"Trillions."

"Oh, okay. Well, let's get everyone up and ready for the hike, okay?"

"Okay."

•••

A couple hours into their hike up the side of a mountain. Jonathan was feeling his heart pound like a hammer. Air was forcing its way through his lungs. Everyone was wearing a backpack filled with supplies and gear.

"This is supposed to be fun?" Rob asked.

"Fun? It's an absolute blast," Blaine replied.

For the most part, Jonathan was quiet during the climb. Clearly, there was a great deal on his mind. Worse off, despite the encouragement he felt earlier, it seemed that he couldn't escape the dream from the night before. Again and again he pictured looking into Albert's eyes for as long as he was able, asking him for the one thing that he could not grant him, the one thing he needed. He felt the desperation and fear of asking, and the pang of rejection. Simply thinking about all of this caused him to have tremors in his hands. But he couldn't stop thinking about it.

"So what to do about Lyla?" Rob asked Jonathan.

"I don't know."

"Well, what do you know?"

"I know that I have to return to my post in a week. That is not a point of negotiation. As much as I'd like to stay here, I can't. Now that I'm being actively hunted by the city of Seattle as well as my old friend, I'm not sure I'd like to stay, anyway. What else do I know? I love spending time with her. When I'm with her, I feel more like a human than at any other time. I feel more complete than I ever did as a star. So, to conclude, I know I want to be with her, and I know that I have to leave. Two contradictory forces."

"Well, could she go with you?"

"What…what do you mean?"

Rob stepped over a large boulder on the ground. "Can she become a star? I mean, mind you, that's assuming that everything worked out and that she was willing. Could she get a contract to be a star? Is that how it works? I'm not really familiar with any of this. I always just thought stars were flaming balls of gas."

Jonathan pointed with a finger as he spoke. "That's a common misconception about stars that humans have. Concerning your point about her becoming a star, the short answer is I don't know. I never thought of that! I suppose I would have to bring it up with the Star Keeper. Do you think he would let her join us? Is there a post for her somewhere in the Milky Way? Do you think? Do you —"

"Calm down, Celesti," Blaine said from the front of the group. "Don't get too excitable; you're hurting the mellow.

"Would you quit calling me that?"

Blaine shrugged. "Why? It has a nice ring to it. It's like an Polish version of you. Who wouldn't want that?"

Rob said, "Sounds more Italian to me…"

"I'm not going to sweat that. I am, however, going to sweat this hike. Let's keep pushing ahead."

The incline only became steeper, the trees taller. They were fully under the cover of a leafy canopy. As was usual, Tim and Mitch were on the quiet, reserved side, saying little except for an occasional remark to each other.

Rob added, "Jonathan. You do need to think about the larger implications of what you are considering. I mean, think about it! You would be asking Lyla to uproot herself from her whole life, from all that she has ever known, so that she could be with you. Friends, family, the city that she loves, all of that gone. It's a lot, Jonathan."

"I know. But I love her, and I think she loves me too. We were meant to be together. Don't' you think that makes it worth it?"

"That's not for me to decide. All I'm saying is that it's not a simple fix."

"But what is the alternative? I get closer to her and it just makes parting hurt all the more. I hated living as a star! Ever since that supernova, hardly any of them will give me the time of day. They treat me like I am less than them. And you know what? I started to believe them. When I came here, it was tough going at first, and Lyla did not exactly leave the greatest first impression. Yet, with time, I have only come to appreciate her more and more. She makes me feel like I am worthwhile, not that I need her to feel that way. It's just, what I'm trying to say is, she brings out the very best in me. She allows me to be the best version of myself. All throughout my time here I have felt dread as I thought about going back to space."

"It sounds like you have really struggled a great deal."

"Ever since that supernova. It was all my fault. I have been unable to escape that event. I have always felt defined by that event. Often, I have wondered how things might be different if it had never happened. Would I feel as broken as I do? Albert says he experienced a lot of suffering. Well, what about me? What about the one who survived?"

"I don't think it's a contest, Jonathan. You know—"

"What about me?! I can barely go a day without my chest aching, my heart pounding, my thoughts racing. I—"

"I know you are hurting, and this is a lot to take in. But things will work out."

"Sure, I just hope I don't end up a white dwarf, or worse, a white sepulcher."

That night, as the others were gathered around a fire, Jonathan was in his tent. By flashlight, he was looking at his book:

Death is when an organism ceases to display the mechanisms that indicate life as humans understand it.

Jonathan recalled how Blaine described death, that it was essentially unknown and unknowable. Philosophies, religions, and other ideologies attempted to make sense of it, to offer comfort. For Jonathan, becoming a white dwarf, or a supernova, was always understood as the way of things. He remembered what Sir Cosmos said, that from every supernova there came the material for a new star to form. Such was not the case with humans. With death, nothing was left, only silence, only emptiness, only coldness. He wondered if death was what Albert had in store for him, whether or not he was even safe out here on the peninsula.

To Jonathan's thinking, this definition of death reflected the inability of humanity or stars to understand what they were grappling with. It was simply beyond the scope of understanding for anyone except perhaps Sir Cosmos, who existed since time immemorial. Yet, even he too would one day fade away, if not for some billions of years.

Alone in the tent, Jonathan became aware of the oppressive darkness all around him. It was cold and quiet. He could hear the faint sounds of the others talking, and see through the tent flap the flickers of the flame's embers.

At one point, Blaine described the Olympic Peninsula as the end of the world, as "untapped". Being from space, this did not terribly impress Jonathan, who throughout millennia explored millions of lightyears of untapped space. Nobody, not even Sir Cosmos, knew where the edge of the universe was, or if there even was one.

Still, there was something beautiful about being on the edge of humanity, in a place where the forces of the natural world thrived. But sitting in the tent in the darkness, Jonathan never before, either as a star or a person, had felt as alone as he did now.

He stepped out of the tent and walked away from the fire. Right now, he wanted to commune with a celestial body. He walked through a row of trees and along a path. The darkness was all-consuming, so he reached out a finger and illuminated his step with it. The branches of the trees were jagged. He nearly bumped into a boulder that was before him. Looking around, knowing it was safe for celestial powers here of all places, he levitated into the air, over the boulder, and found himself in a clearing, a meadow.

He walked up the slope of the meadow, to the top of a gentle, rolling hill. On the ground he lay down, looking up at the stars of the night. He closed his eyes and called out:

North Star, are you there?

Greetings, Jonathan. What is your status?

Tell me, North Star, what is the path I am to take?

Calculations indicate a path due west of here to arrive at the campground.

No. I mean, what am I supposed to do?

In approximately 1,000 feet, you will reach your destination.

Is Sir Cosmos around?

`Presently he is occupied attending to other matters.

North Star, when will the stars of the night sky forgive me for what happened all those years ago? When will they treat me like one of their own?

Calculations suggest an 80% chance that—

At that moment, Jonathan heard the voices of many different stars speaking.

Several stars flew down from the sky and hovered around Jonathan.

Victoria, Maxwell, Skyler! I haven't seen you in millions of years!

Jonathan. Though what you did a billion years ago was awful, it was awful of us to treat you so unkindly. It didn't make anything better; it only created more hurt. Please forgive us as we forgive you!

Of course I forgive you.

And the way that Albert is treating you…it is terrible indeed. Here, let us lift you up so you can see things from a different perspective.

The three stars floated to the side, and another dozen stars appeared. All the stars came around Jonathan, gripping him, lifting him high up into the air. His body was glowing with a luminous light, each star flashing like a crystalline diamond that twinkled continuously.

High up in the air, Jonathan looked and saw the tapestry of constellations. All at once, he felt the hatred and bitterness inside him towards these celestial bodies melt away. Once more he heard the voices:

We're sorry, Jonathan!

Didn't mean to make you feel so bad.

Please forgive us.

We can't wait for you to come back and be with us.

We're proud of everything you have done.

Jonathan felt the love of his comrades, as he replied:

I'm so sorry about what happened all those years ago. Believe me, I am doing what I can to make things right now. The support you are all showing me means the world to me. It means the world and everything that goes beyond it!

For a few more minutes Jonathan communed with the stars. A question was on his mind:

What prompted you, after a billion years of unkindness, to forgive me?

Skyler replied:

I think it was finding out what Albert has done to you. That put things in perspective, and it made us realize where we went wrong.

Slowly, Jonathan hovered back down to the ground. Smiling, he thought that, for the first time since he could remember, it just might not be so bad to go back to being a star again.

Day 24

Walking on a sunny day, the group was making their way along the cusp of the water. In the distance, there were grassy hills that rose higher and higher until they formed cliffs overlooking the wild waters. But these hills were a long ways off, and it would be a while before the group reached even their beginning.

Standing at the bottom of the hills, the friends looked at one another, and proceeded to walk up the slope. Already the view of the sea was becoming more expansive. Sea gulls flew overhead. The wind rustled the tips of grass. To Jonathan, it felt quite tranquil.

"Look at those hills! Breathtaking! Stunning! Deeply, utterly affecting!" Jonathan cried.

The others didn't look at him as he spoke.

"The created world is something to marvel at," Jonathan continued.

"Yeah," Blaine replied. "Sure is. What do you want to do about Albert?" Blaine asked.

Jonathan paused. "I'm not sure."

"Well, that's the problem."

"I think, if I could just get close to him without being attacked, if I looked him in the eyes and apologized, he might stop all of this."

"Do you really think it's that easy?"

"I don't know. On the other hand, I could find Lyla, convince her to become a star with me, and escape from this planet. Like I said, I'm not sure."

"That sounds a little more realistic. Except for the part where Lyla becomes a star. That doesn't sound very realistic."

"If I can get the Star Keeper's permission, then yes, it is."

"The way I see it, Albert is full of a consuming rage. When someone becomes that hurt, that full of anger, they lose the ability to see clearly, and nothing is going to open their eyes. At least that's what I think."

"So you think I should just escape with Lyla?"

"I'm not going to tell you what to do, but I will say that I think approaching Albert is very, very dangerous."

"I agree. He is a very powerful star."

"Indeed," Blaine replied.

"All I desire," Jonathan spoke, "is life in its pure self, and nothing less. That's why I need to escape. Now that I think about it, it's obvious that being forgiven by him is out of the question."

Blaine said, "It sounds like you have decided, then: grab the girl and run off. This, of course, assumes that she will be willing."

"I sure hope she is."

They continued walking for a while in silence.

"Always nice to get out into nature, to escape," Blaine eventually said.

"Is it escaping?" Rob challenged. "To me, it feels more like returning, like coming home from the madness that is life in Seattle."

"Fair enough, friend. Fair enough."

"It is nice to get away from the rat race, though, isn't it?" Rob asked.

"What?"

Blaine laughed. Then he turned to Jonathan and said, "Like a lot of things, it's an expression. The Rat Race… hmm, how to put it? I suppose it describes the endless human struggle to have more."

"More of what?"

Rob said, "A nicer car, a prettier spouse, a bigger house, a better job, you name it. Humans were made to pine for things."

"Often people work so hard to obtain all of these things for the express purpose of making their friends and peers feel bad or inferior," Blaine added.

"That seems harmful," Jonathan said.

Rob said, "It's human nature."

"Say more about that."

"One thing at a time," Blaine replied as he jumped onto a log and carefully walked along it. "The Rat Race is essentially marked by futility. It's all about climbing the ladder, 'getting ahead', etc. But to what end? All that comes from it is death. That's why it's called the Rat Race. It's a lot like looking down on a couple of animals locked in a struggle to be the best, unaware that none of it really matters."

Jonathan asked, "You sound like the moon. What does matter, then?"

"You tell us," Rob replied.

Jonathan ran a hand through his hair. "Well, last night, at long last, I was reconciled to the stars in my galaxy."

"That's great to hear!" Blaine said. He was still walking on the log.

The base of the hills was no longer far off. The sea was like a painting, unmoving, constant, a backdrop to the conversation.

Jonathan said, "I don't have a lot. I have no money. I have three shirts and two pairs of pants. But I have a voice, and this body that I walk around in, and you know what? That's a lot!" There was a pause. "But now, all of that is at stake. What do I do?"

Jonathan continued, saying, "Here we have been here for several days, and I don't feel like I have made any progress when it comes to figuring out what to do about Albert."

They passed by a lone boulder that sat on the trail. Jonathan jumped and scaled the boulder with ease.

"Guys!" he spoke. "The view up here is unimaginable."

"I think we can imagine," Blaine answered. "Now come down here."

Onwards they walked, the trail winding higher up.

Blaine sighed, and then said, "It seems to me in our culture that there is a particular narrative that is pretty firmly in place: go to college, get a job, get married, have kids, grow old, die. It's all so…passé. I mean, that sort of thing is fine for other people, but not for me."

"What part of the trajectory did you complete?" Jonathan asked.

"Well, I went to school. I got a job, while not a salaried one, and I did meet a girl, but we parted ways. Yes, I think that my music holds a more special place in my heart. I just love to make it. Being that sort of person means that I don't fit snugly into the boxes that our culture is creating."

Rob said, "I went to college, never met a girl, but did build up a pretty good network of contacts for my video and design projects. What can Blaine and I say? We're artists; we aren't businessmen."

"Is acting art?"

"Yes," Blaine said.

"Then I'm an artist, too. How cool is that?"

"Pretty freaking cool," Blaine replied.

Now they were standing at a clearing. Behind them was a meadow. Before them was the sea, which seemed distant now, yet swallowed up everything in the horizon.

Jonathan turned to face Blaine. "Have you ever aspired to reproduce?" he asked him.

The group laughed. Blaine said, "No…having kids just isn't for me."

"Why?"

"I don't know, it's just not in my nature."

"Stars are boring. We just form and then fade. No elaborate bodily exchanges."

"You really have a way with words," Blaine said.

"Let's talk about the nature of humans!" Jonathan said.

"What about the nature?" Rob asked inquisitively.

Jonathan opened his mouth and recited an entry from his book:

> *Theologians, historians, philosophers, poets, politicians, and thinkers of all sorts has sought to answer this question: is man inherently good? While some believe humanity to be fundamentally corrupted, or fallen, others consider it to be benevolent and righteous, striving for great things. There is little consensus on this issue. To make the conversation still more problematic, there are people who fall in between these two camps, offering shades of gray to the mixture. Indeed, the destiny and fate of man is a difficult one for us to discuss. Further inquiry into—*

"Okay," Blaine interjected, "I get what you mean. Boy, that book has a way of being verbose."

"What do you mean by 'verbose'?" Jonathan asked.

"Using an excessive amount of words to convey something."

"Oh, well why didn't you use that instead?"

"Because I like to use the word verbose to avoid being verbose."

"Oh…I see."

"Anyway," Blaine said, "I think humanity is fundamentally flawed and broken, and I see no solution, other than to always strive to better ourselves. Mistakes will be made, but progress is possible."

"So do you think humanity is evil?"

"Um…I don't know if that's the right word. Given how history has played out, I definitely think that we are corrupted in some form."

"I agree," Rob said, "but I hold that, through learning to live for and to serve God, it is possible to find redemption, to be made new."

"Oh," Jonathan replied. "I think humanity, from what I have seen and read, is good. We are good! We are meant for good things and we accomplish good things."

Blaine and Rob looked at each other.

In the distance they saw a fellow hang gliding.

"I want to try!" Jonathan exclaimed.

He ran towards a tent, where they were offering to let people pay to hang glide.

"Can we do it, please?" Jonathan begged Blaine.

"You can do it."

"But doing things together makes them better. Sharing is the key to enjoyment. Come on, you'll get to feel what it's like to fall to earth as a star."

"No, I, you know..."

But Blaine saw in Jonathan Celestial's eyes a purity of heart that could not be denied. He knew he had to go hang gliding.

They paid the price and walked towards the edge of the cliff. While Blaine was looking down at the sharp, jagged rocks below, Jonathan was gazing out towards the lolling waves in the distance.

"I don't know about this—"

"Let's go!"

Jonathan ran, and they jumped off the cliff. Through the air they soared, the sound of Jonathan laughing and screaming filling the air. Blaine, too, was screaming, but in terror rather than joy.

Below them, beneath their feet, there seemed to be the whole world. Jonathan admired the Earth from his post as a star innumerable times, and he flew and floated through the heavens just as much, but there was something about gliding with someone who had never done it that was so refreshing for him, so very vital. Jonathan knew he had nothing. He had no money and hardly any clothes, but he did have his friends, as well as the love of his twenty-three-day-long life. In this sense, he had everything in the world. It was all his.

They drifted with the wind currents, slowly lowering themselves towards the shore below. Around them there were other hang gliders.

Now somewhat collected, Blaine said, "This is amazing, Jonathan. Is this what it feels like to be a star?"

"Pretty much!"

"Well, consider me interested in signing up."

Finally they reached the shore, where their friends were waiting. Jonathan stuck out his feet and prepared for the landing. It was a bit awkward, but the hang glider was undamaged, and no one was hurt.

"How was it?" Rob asked.

"It was awesome!" Blaine shouted. This was the first time Jonathan heard Blaine's voice rise above the soft tone it usually rested at.

"I'm afraid we'll need to head back now," Blaine said. "I don't know what we can expect to find in Seattle, but you've had some time to reflect and grow a bit. You went on your first trip!"

"And what a trip it was!"

"And now we have a plan: talk to the Star Keeper about returning to space with the girl, all without being caught by the evil star impersonating an Agent. What could be simpler?"

Back at the camp ground, Jonathan had a chance to think inside the tent. He knew that danger was right around the corner, but he also knew that there was a greater, more mighty voice that demanded he live his life. Jonathan picked up his book, leafing through it, and then decided that there was a better way to spend his time. He walked outside the tent, to where a view of the ocean was afforded, the breeze blowing at his back, and he breathed in deeply only to exhale.

DAY 25

They arrived late at night. Nervous, Jonathan Celestial stepped outside, looking up at the night sky which looked all the more inviting to him with each passing night. Jonathan closed his eyes:

Hello, Star Keeper?

Jonathan Celestial. What are you doing talking to us during your paid time off? Shouldn't you be off, running about, doing whatever it is that humans do?

I thought I'd take a moment to ask you something.

Well, what is it?

I, um…um…

Jonathan?

I was wondering if there might be a way…you see, there's this girl…

Ah, but of course! A girl. Jonathan Celestial: Ladies' man. What do you want? I think I know where this is going.

I was hoping she could become a star and live with me in the cosmos for the next couple billion of years.

You know, we stars have been watching your ventures rather carefully, Jonathan. In particular, we have been watching how Albert has been hunting you. It's rather sickening. Of course what you did to him was awful. It was—

I don't want to go into what I did. I wanted to talk to you about where I am going.

But Jonathan—

The supernova was a billion years ago. Surely you can let it go?

Now, Jonathan, I know the stars of this galaxy have come to embrace you and all, but I remain wary.

Maybe, as the Star Keeper, you might benefit from following the lead of the stars for once instead of always being the boss.

That is no way to talk to your superior!

It would seem that it in fact is, seeing as how I just said it.

So, Jonathan, you disrespect me and the office I have, and then you have the audacity to request of me that I grant starhood to your girlfriend?

She loves stars. Not just me. She loves space and the cosmos. I think she'd fit in great.

Well, give me a moment Jonathan…yes, here it is. According to The Code of the Stars: Policy and Procedure Manual, 1,762nd edition: "A human may be granted starhood if she is willing, specifically, if she wishes on a star that she might become one." Well, there you go.

So if she wants to be a star she can be one?!

That's what it says, Jonathan. I don't think it has ever actually happened in cosmic memory, but it is possible. After all, you are the first star to come to Earth. Previously, it was untapped, a final frontier of sorts.

I will talk to her.

Sure thing, Jonathan. I just have one important question.

What?

How is her work ethic?

Stellar!

Okay. You have your conversation with her.

Walking back inside the apartment, he went into the main room and had a seat at the table.

The phone rang.

Apprehensive, he wiped a drop of sweat from his forehead and picked up the receiver. Every call could be from him.

"Hello?"

"Hey, Jonathan. What are you doing?"

"Oh, hi Lyla. Just communing with the created world."

"Sounds self-aggrandizing. What are you doing in two days?"

"Meeting with you?"

"Precisely. I say we meet at the Overlake Observatory and spend some time looking at the stars, you know, to commune with the created world."

"Sounds great!"

"Good."

"Listen, Lyla."

"Yes?"

"There's something very important I have to talk to about with you."

"Okay…"

"I'll leave it there until we meet up. I'll see you soon."

"See you soon."

Jonathan climbed into bed. Blaine was visiting a friend and said he wouldn't be back until late. Jonathan felt an aching sensation in his chest, as though his ribs were shaking. His heart was beating rapidly. His breathing was short and shallow. He thought about disclosing his identity to Lyla. Would she still want to be around him? Would she still want to hold his hand?

Anxiety, panic, the feeling that he couldn't handle being in that moment seized him. He rose from the bed and looked out the window.

Walking outside, he found a star and made a wish:

I wish that Lyla would be willing to become a star and spend the rest of her life with me.

He saw the star he was watching twinkle, signifying it received his wish.

Hello Jonathan,

Sounds like you're in love. We will be working on your wish, but bear in mind that the will of sentient beings goes beyond the scope of the wishes we typically grant. We'll see what we can do. Wishers who made a wish like yours also wished for: chocolate, better sleep, and the latest movies. Close your eyes and wish to learn more. Sincerely, Mason from the Star Department of Wishes and Whimsies

Unsettled, Jonathan climbed back into the bed. Tossing and turning, he thought about Albert, about how he didn't want to leave Earth and be with Lyla until he obtained forgiveness from him. But he didn't know if it would be possible to be reconciled. In his mind, he saw the hatred, which was really just a shield for the hurt underlying it, and at once he knew that there was nothing he could do to control the will of another, sentient being. Still, he felt the desire to at least approach him.

Then he imagined death, utter annihilation, a fate as bad as being a white dwarf.

He didn't know what to do. All he knew was that he was dreading talking to Lyla. She was on his side. She cared for him, and he feared losing that, being left with a former friend who wanted to destroy him.

No one ever told Jonathan how difficult being a human could be.

DAY 26

Nervous, Jonathan Celestial waited at the base of Overlake Observatory. He was kicking rocks off the path and into the grassy field below. Situated at the top of the hill that was Volunteer Park, the observatory was ostensibly the definitive way to look at the stars, apart from simply being a star and occupying space.

Racing through Jonathan's mind was the familiar crippling anxiety of letting another human know him as he truly was. For so long, for a billion years, he wore armor to protect himself. He didn't talk about the things that hurt him, but they accompanied him, regardless, ghosts hovering over the surface of the water.

"How will she respond?" he whispered.

His time was short. He needed to make it count. But moreover, he needed to find a way to make his life as a human count. He didn't want to survive; he wanted to do something more.

Then he saw her.

She was wearing a black and white dress with a retro hat. In a word, she was lovely. As he watched her walk up the steps towards him, he realized how profoundly he wanted to be with her, to be with her for all time.

"Hi, handsome," she said in a breathy voice.

"Beautiful! You look positively gorgeous! Er, I apologize for being overly intense. How are you, Lyla?"

"I am well," she said in a gentle tone. "Are you ready to look at some constellations?"

"Yes! Oh, boy, yes!"

Together they went up the stairs to the observatory. Inside, there were rainbow-colored lights shining upwards, providing a fun ambience. There were a few people, walking around, looking at the models of the planets and stars. Jonathan went towards the telescope in the center of the room.

"Here, you go first."

She looked through the telescope.

"What do you see?" he asked.

"Leo…and I think, Cancer."

"Can I take a look?"

Jonathan put an eye against the telescope. This was, by his estimation, the absolutely worst way he had ever observed the stars of the sky, but out of fondness for her he pretended to be in awe of what he saw.

"Let's see…Libra….Cervus….Crater…Hydra…Virgo…"

"You're really good at this, aren't you?" she said.

"I love the stars."

"I know. I do, too. But it seems like you have a special bond with them, like you connect with them."

Jonathan looked around the strange observatory and then turned to face her.

"Here, follow me." He took her hand in his and they went back outside.

Standing at the bottom of the steps, it was so dark that they could hardly see a thing save the tapestry of celestial bodies above.

Jonathan looked at her, seeing her for her beautiful self.

"You have an eyelash," he said, and he removed it.

"Thanks," she said.

A pause followed, then she asked, "Now, why on earth did you lead me out here? We were just getting started.

Jonathan reached out both of his hands. "Here, take my hands; close your eyes."

"What are you—"

"Just trust me."

She did as he instructed. Holding her hands in his, he was struck by how warm they were. Gently, slowly, he enabled the two of them to hover up into the air. Higher and higher they went, until they were on top of the observatory. Because it was so dark no one was able to see them.

They sat on the dome of the observatory, all of outer space spread out before them.

"Now this," he said, "is a view."

"I would have to agree. But how did you get us up here? That was unreal!"

"Lyla…"

"What?"

"I need to tell you something. I don't know how to say this, but—"

"Oh, are you talking about how you are a star?"

Jonathan's jaw lowered. "How…how…"

Lyla put a hand on his shoulder. "Your name is Jonathan Celestial. You appeared shortly after the crater formed. You are poor with social cues."

"I am," Jonathan replied. "I am what people have been calling the alien. A long time ago, I led my best friend into a supernova. I know it sounds stupid, and that's because it is. I was then ostracized by my community. I knew that I had to do whatever I could to find a new start. So I worked, following the leadership of the Star Keeper. I worked for a billion years, and finally I accrued enough PTO to come to Earth and try being a human. They warned me, telling me that this was an awful place, but I came anyway, because I had faith that I would find the source of something that might bring me out of darkness…some light. My time here has been wild. Lots of coffee, living with the guitarist of a band, working as an actor, swimming in the Pacific Ocean, almost dying in a car crash, hang gliding. It's been a wonderful, wonderful time! I've also had loads of conversations with my friends, and learned more about the things that you humans struggle with. I guess that's my story. Well, of course, I forgot to mention how I met you, and how I knew at once that I loved you. I love you! I just feel so thankful that I've had the opportunity to be a human. I will always be thankful for that.

"Jonathan…"

"What is it, Lyla?"

She leaned in and whispered in his ear, "I love you, too." She kissed him on the lips.

Jonathan placed his hands on her face. He kissed her with everything he had. For the first time in all those years, it felt like the supernova was erased, completely gone.

"But you aren't a menace," she said with a laugh. "All you want to do is live, to spread cheer and kindness. I don't know how the Agent hunting you could be so wrong about you. Wait…yes I do. It's the government: they tend to get things wrong."

"I don't know either. But what I do know is that my time here on Earth is short. But I care about you, and I don't want to be apart from you. It makes me feel an ache in my chest just thinking about it!"

"So what do you have in mind?"

"I want you to come with me, to be a star."

"What the—"

"You don't have to answer right now. You can think about it. I just wanted to offer it to you, because I always want to be with you." He leaned in towards her and kissed her on the lips once more.

She looked at him, as though she were surveying his entire body. "The city has been in a panic for weeks, the newspapers saying that a celestial monster is dwelling among us, and it turns out to be the guy I am seeing? It's all comical, really."

"When did you know I was a star?"

Lyla put a hand across her chest, on her shoulder. "Me? I knew there was something otherworldly about you the minute I first sat with you at that café table. You were just so…weird."

Jonathan breathed in deeply. "The truth is I am in real danger. If he catches me, I know he'll kill me. Then there won't be any time working under the Star Keeper or being with Sir Cosmos. You and I will be separated."

"I don't know how to assimilate any of what I'm hearing. Who are they? My graduate Astronomy textbook never mentioned them."

"It may be hard to believe, but it's the truth."

Jonathan looked around, and then said to her, "Let me show you something."

He rose up into the air. For a moment he hovered there. Then, he whistled. Stars appeared all around him. They proceeded to circle him at high speeds, swirling faster and faster. They left behind trails of light. Soon, he was encircled in light.

"Okay, boys!"

He snapped his fingers, and all the stars came to a halt. They rested in place, and then soared high up into the heavens.

Jonathan fell back down to the observatory roof.

"We stars are all friends. We live in peace and harmony. Well, for a billion years they hardly talked to me, but everything is better now. Sometimes stars can be cruel and unkind, it's true. But for the most part, we are good folk. And I'm convinced that humanity is good, too."

"But humanity thinks you're a monster!"

"I know, that's why I want you to go with me back to space, to escape. I came here because I wanted to be cleansed from the hurt I inflicted on Albert. Now I know with all my being that there's no hope for that. He is possessed by anger and rage. He will kill me at all costs."

"Yes," she replied, "and you need to go to him."

Jonathan shrunk back. "What?"

Lyla shrugged. "You need to turn yourself in, to approach him."

"No, I can't."

She put a hand on his shoulder. "Jonathan, you can't live in fear. You should go to him. Ask him for forgiveness, again. If he destroys you, well, I don't think that will happen. Approach him and I think he will appreciate it. Do it for me. Do it for him. Most of all, do it for yourself."

"I can't just go walk up to him and ask him to forgive me for nearly killing him."

"It's a weird idea," she said smiling, "but you're a weird guy. Look, Jonathan, you came here to Earth for a reason. You can't leave now. You originally came to find some space from things. But guess what! The one you want to find forgiveness from is still alive! Think about how many people never get to be reconciled to those who have hurt them until it's too late. What this is, really, is an opportunity. Even if he tries to hurt you, well I think you will get through to him."

"You do?"

She nodded. "And as for the whole star thing...I don't really know how I feel about that. It's pretty bizarre. How does that work, logistically speaking? Can I still wear cute dresses?

"I want us to be together always."

"But what you need to think about is what I would be leaving behind to be with you. I have my family, my friends, my education. It's so much. I guess what I am trying to say is that I feel to weighed down to just float into the air and be a star. Would I even like being a star? I feel like I hardly know you."

Jonathan was looking at the floor. "It hurts me to think that you wouldn't want to join me in the night sky. There is a life waiting for us. There is so much waiting for us. Promise me that you will consider it."

She looked at him intently. "I'll consider it. But to be honest, I really don't know what to think right now."

There was a pause. Together, they looked up at the stars. Jonathan pointed out each and every constellation and star, referring to them by name. His knowledge for this sort of thing was boundless because he was talking about his home, his friends.

Eventually she turned to look at him. "You need to go to him."

Jonathan was looking upward. "I don't know. I don't know what to do."

"You need to—"

"I need to run!" Jonathan was breathing heavily. "He will rip me apart!"

"I can't stop you from running away to space. But I know you spent a billion years wishing you could make things right. This is your chance."

Jonathan taught her more about stars, about their culture, how they danced, and sang. Later on, when the sun was not far away, he brought her and he back down to the ground, in a corner behind trees and bushes.

Parting, he kissed her one more time. "Think about it," he said. "Consider being a star. It's really a pretty great way to be!"

"Consider talking to the Agent…consider the possibility of a second chance."

"That is not my choice to make."

"I suppose you're right."

Jonathan walked back across the city, towards his home. Inside, he saw Blaine was reading a book and drinking coffee.

"How did it go?"

"I need to be alone.

Jonathan went to his room and opened his book, but he found that, as was often the case, he was less than engaged in the reading. He went to the window and saluted the Sun. Then he came back out into the main space.

"You do know there's a party tonight, don't you?" Blaine asked.

"Oh, yes."

"Should be a good time."

Jonathan nodded. But inside, all he felt was confusion as he thought about the love of his life and the wrath of someone who had been a friend.

DAY 27

Jonathan Celestial walked out the door of the *Eclipse* apartment. He could hear the sounds of people chanting. His instinct was to move in the opposite direction, but then he remembered what his objective was. Moving towards the voices, he saw Henrietta, who led one of the groups against his presence.

"So there he is!" she shouted.

"Here I am."

She walked towards him. She looked at his feet, then at his face. "Are you, are you going to try to annihilate me?" she asked.

Jonathan smiled. "No, I just want to talk to your boss."

"Grab him," she said to two burly men standing nearby. They took him by his arms, gripping him tightly. They walked towards the Bureau office, Jonathan in no way resisting. Henrietta was smiling, and continued to look at Jonathan.

"I can't believe it was that easy to capture him. Willows is going to be so pleased!"

They moved slowly. At a busy intersection they stopped. On the other side of the street was a counter-demonstration group, led by Dave.

"There he is!" Dave pointed. "We must save the righteous cosmic presence."

Dave led his group over, and they proceeded to clash with Henrietta's group. Demonstrators were yelling and fighting, punching and kicking. In all the confusion, the two men who had been holding Jonathan were gone.

He sighed slowly.

Dave approached Jonathan. "Aren't you going to escape, enlightened one? Aren't you going to ascend back to the cosmos?"

"Don't think so." Jonathan brushed past Dave and continued walking towards the office.

"He's going to the office!" someone shouted.

Dave raised a hand. "Let him go."

"But, leader—"

"If he is meant to return to the lab, then who are we to judge the will of this most benevolent cosmic presence?"

The members of Dave's group nodded in deep admiration as they watched Jonathan walk up the steps to the office. Jonathan banged on the door with a closed fist.

"Who is it?" a guard asked.

"Jonathan Celestial. I'd like to speak with Gray Willows."

"Okay. But shouldn't you be on the run or something?"

"No, there can be no more running."

"Whatever you say, Mr. Celestial."

The door opened. Jonathan moved up the stairs and through the hallway. He didn't stop to acknowledge Bernice. He approached the massive doors to Willows' office. Once more, he banged on them with a fist.

"Let me in, Gray."

The door opened. Gray Willows stood, looking at Jonathan incredulously. "Can it really be you?"

"It's me. I'm here so you can do what you need to do."

"What's that mean?"

"You said you wanted me to suffer like you did, so here I am. I'm ready to suffer."

Gray's face widened in a grin. "Right this way, Jonathan."

Led into a different jail cell, Jonathan noticed that there were no windows, no way to commune with the celestial bodies. He heard the sound of the cell door close behind him.

"I'll deal with you tomorrow," Gray said. "Don't worry; it will be a grand spectacle. Everyone will see how I got justice from watching you writhe."

"Sure thing."

Gray leaned in closely. "Just so you know: I don't trust you. Not in the slightest. I know you are up to something, and that's why I'm leaving you in this dark room. Nothing but you and your thoughts to keep you company."

"Okay, Albert—"

"Don't call me that!" he screamed. "I'm Agent Gray Willows. Albert as you knew him is gone." He turned off the light switch. "Sleep well; it may be your last chance."

"All right, Gray."

Jonathan sat there in the cell. He reached out a finger and used it to illuminate the space. He looked at the light pouring forth from his finger.

"Even here… in the dark… there is light."

DAY 28

"You're still here."

Jonathan Celestial didn't sleep at all the entire night. The lights startled him as they came on. In a daze, he looked at Gray and saw the same grin from before.

"I'm still here."

"Did you sleep well?"

"No, in fact I didn't."

"So sorry to hear." Gray opened the door. Behind him stood two guards. "Come with me."

Jonathan followed them up a pair of stairs, into his office. Gray walked over to the book shelf and pulled on the dictionary. The bookshelf rotated, revealing a hidden passage.

"Nobody works on their lexicon these days," Gray said.

They went up more stairs and were soon on the roof of the building, several floors above the streets. Helicopters were floating overhead, under the cloudy sky which blotted everything out. Beneath the building people were gathered.

"There he is!" a voice called from below.

All at once the roaring sound of the crowd was overwhelming. Voices were calling out many different messages:

"Set him free!"

"Kill the alien!"

"Study him to find a cure for disease!"

The guard on Jonathan's left punched him, causing him to fall to the ground. The guard then placed a boot on his chest. Jonathan was shaking.

Gray walked over and gestured with his hand. "I thought I'd bring some special guests to today's event."

Looking up, Jonathan saw that Lyla, Blaine, and Rob were standing nearby, with several guards gathered around them.

"What in the—"

"They're here, to watch justice unfold," Gray said. He walked over and picked up a taser.

Jonathan looked at Gray. "Albert..." he said.

"Don't call me that!" He slapped Jonathan who turned to look away, quivering. Then Jonathan turned to look into Gray's eyes. "I need to call you by that name. I need to make things right."

"You want to make things right? Then you will have to pay the price." He leaned in close to look at Jonathan. There was wrath in his eyes. "You have no idea how much pain I felt, how alone I felt after it happened. I still can't sleep at night. You..." Gray leaned in closer. "You have no idea at all."

"I understand that that is how you feel. I won't try to invalidate any of that."

"Oh, so you think by playing cute therapist you can avoid what's to come, do you?"

Jonathan shook his head, and said with a soft voice, "I'm sorry. Whatever you need to do, go ahead and do it. I just want to be..."

"Be what?"

Jonathan looked up at the sky. "I just want to be your friend again. What I did all those millions of years ago was...you know what it was. I just miss floating through space with you, talking about all the things we wanted to do. I just want to be with you again."

Gray lowered himself down so that he was looking straight into Jonathan's eyes. "It's too late for that. Things will never be the way they were." He shouted, "I'm not who I was anymore! You made me into who I am!"

A pause followed. Blaine, Lyla, and Rob stood, the guards closely surrounding them.

Jonathan and Gray were looking intently at one another. Jonathan said softly, "Albert…"

Albert answered, "What?"

Jonathan stammered. "Forgive…forgive me."

Albert said quickly, "No! I don't forgive you! Stop it! Enough of this." He grabbed the taser, pointed it at Jonathan, and fired it.

A loud scream sounded.

There was a flash. Sparks were soaring through the air. The body was shaking as it absorbed the blast. The body shook, and then it fell to the ground.

On the ground, laying still, was Blaine.

Jonathan looked at him. He opened his mouth to scream, but nothing came out.

Tears fell from Lyla's eyes. She looked away.

Holding the taser, Albert looked at the body on the ground, then at Jonathan, then at the guards, then back at the body. Violently, he threw the taser on the ground and began to sob.

Jonathan reached out a hand, but Albert slapped it away.

His hands in his face, Albert said, "How could I…" Then he whispered, "what am I doing?"

"It's okay," Jonathan said.

"No it's not!" Albert shouted. "I came here to make you feel what I felt, and all I ended up doing was hurting this…this…"

"Friend of mine," Jonathan finished.

"Yes, this friend of yours." Albert picked up the taser and turned it off. "To have a friend who would do something like that…who would take a blow for you…that must feel pretty good."

Jonathan reached out a hand. "I understand if you don't forgive me. I accept that. I just wanted to make things right. I wanted the same thing as you."

Albert wiped several tears from his eyes. "How do we do that? It's too late to make things right."

Jonathan smiled. "As long as there is breath in our lungs, it isn't too late. Do you forgive me?"

Blaine rolled over and looked up at the two of them, groaning in pain.

Slowly, Albert reached out a hand and took Jonathan's in his own.

The two of them smiled.

DAY 29

They walked along the beach, laughing, recounting their days at the Star Academy. The tide gently graced their feet. Standing by the waves, Jonathan smiled and waved as his friend Albert floated up into the heavens, back into space.

DAY 30

In truth, there was not a lot to be said regarding Jonathan Celestial's final day as a human.

Static Sea was having a concert, performing in the crater at Volunteer Park. Blaine was excited to be trying out some new songs. Jonathan was even invited up to sing for a few of the numbers. The crowd was in awe of his voice.

In light of what happened days before, the city had settled down. Blaine, Albert, Jonathan, and Lyla spoke to the newspaper about stars, how friendly and benign they were, and quickly the popular opinion of them became more accepting.

So there were local coffee stands set up throughout the park. People from the city were gathered to see Jonathan off.

Between singing songs, Jonathan found Lyla.

"Hi, Lyla, I need to explain. I, er—"

"You don't need to explain anything," she said. "Listen, I did a lot of thinking in the last couple of days. I have things that tie me here to Earth: my family, my friends, my education, all that stuff. But I figure, if I can be a star, then I can be with you for a long, long time, and I can look down on my friends and family. I can be a source of reassurance and warmth for them!"

"What you just said is beautiful! So you mean it? You want to be a star?"

"I do!"

They hugged, and then kissed.

Later, Jonathan approached Blaine.

"What you did up there on the rooftop for me…it was incredible! How can I thank you?"

"Jonathan Celestial. Boy, does it feel nice to be able to talk to you as a star in the open, in safety. How can I thank you? You keep talking about having been in a dark place. Well, I was in a dark place of my own, and you shone a light into it."

"Well, I am a star!"

Blaine hugged him. "I'm gonna miss you."

Still later on, Jonathan found Rob.

"I just wanted you to know," he said, "I think that your belief in God is a beautiful thing. I don't know if He exists, but I do know that I have really valued your friendship. I wish you the best. And I hope that I can encourage you in your journey with anxiety; it will get better."

"Thanks, Jonathan!"

They celebrated all the day long. As night came, Jonathan closed his eyes, standing next to Lyla.

"What are you doing?" she asked.

"Close your eyes."

Hello, Star Keeper?

Hello, Jonathan.

Star Keeper, this is Lyla.

Lyla, that's a lovely name. Reminds me of the constellation, Lyra. Very well-run.

Hello, Mr. Star Keeper.

Hello, Lyla. So you want to be a star, eh?

Yes!

Well, okay. All right. I suppose we can find a post for you. You and Jonathan will be sent to the same galaxy. Just make sure to keep things professional at work!

Of course! Haven't I always been professional in my billion years of service?

You have. Okay then. I suppose I can file away your wish as granted, Jonathan?

I think so!

And with that, Jonathan Celestial and Lyla said one final goodbye to those close to them. Beams of light shone down, and they floated up into the night sky, drifting off to their posts. Though Jonathan and Blaine would never see each other as humans, the fact remained that Jonathan, with Lyla at his side, would shine light and radiate warmth to Earth for billions of years to come.

About the Author

Sean Anderson is an author who lives near Seattle. In his free time, he enjoys meditating, being in nature, and going for walks with his wife. He is the author of The Year of Oceans and The Celestial Life.

If you enjoyed this book, please consider leaving an online review. The author would appreciate reading your thoughts.

You can also follow the author on social media

Twitter
https://twitter.com/Sean_T_Anderson

FaceBook
https://www.facebook.com/SeanThomasAnderson/

ABOUT THE PUBLISHER

Sulis International Press publishes fine fiction and nonfiction in a variety of genres.

For more, visit the website at
https://sulisinternational.com
Subscribe to the newsletter at
https://sulisinternational.com/subscribe/

Follow on social media
https://www.facebook.com/SulisInternational
https://twitter.com/Sulis_Intl
https://www.pinterest.com/Sulis_Intl/
https://www.instagram.com/sulis_international/

www.ingramcontent.com/pod-product-compliance
Lightning Source LLC
Chambersburg PA
CBHW050517190726
48284CB00003B/846